SOLOMON ISLAND FOLKTALES
from Malaita

Solomon Island Folktales
from Malaita

Collected and translated by Kay Bauman

Rutledge Books, Inc.  Danbury, CT

Front cover photo: Village elder Lebefiu wearing shell valuables and holding a *subi* club.

Back cover photo: Two girls making loud drum-like sounds using only their hands in the water, called *ki kafo*.

Copyright© 1998 by Kay Bauman

ALL RIGHTS RESERVED
Rutledge Books, Inc.
107 Mill Plain Road, Danbury, CT 06811
1-800-278-8533

Manufactured in the United States of America

Cataloging in Publication Data
Bauman, Kay
   Soloman Island folktales from Malaita

   ISBN: 1-887750-77-0

   1. Folktales. 2. Tales. I. Title

398.08   97-69557

Dedicated to

Micah Sedea and Lebefiu

For Linda,
Thank you for
all your hard
work on this.
Kay.
April 1998

ACKNOWLEDGMENTS

The field trip to Malaita would not have been possible without the guidance and encouragement of Dr. Douglas Oliver, my first husband Harold Ross's Ph.D. advisor in anthropology at Harvard University. A research grant from the National Institute of Mental Health financially supported this project.

My thanks also to Harold Ross without whom I would not have traveled to Malaita. Our two oldest children, Ted and Anne, then seven and two years old, made our entry into this culture much swifter since the Malaitans adore children. Our third child Dave was indirectly responsible for my preparing this material for publication.

Linda Syfert Platten carefully put the typed manuscript on computer. My husband, Walter Bauman, gave me the time and encouragement to complete this work. Finally, I thank the people of Malaita who shared their ideas and way of life with us.

Contents

Foreword xi

Introduction xiii

Maps xxi

Photos xxv

Origins 1

Fools 19

Women 25

Heroes 59

Black Magic 83

Recent Clan Warfare 89

The Pig Beukwalangia 93

Bibliography 99

FOREWORD

Hats off to Mrs. Kay Bauman!

In 1966, with no prior experience of the kind, she and their two small children accompanied her graduate-student husband to the unfrequented interior of a remote Solomon Island and remained there in a native village for over a year — making a home for her family, keeping them healthy, and assisting her husband in his anthropological research (which eventuated in an outstanding book on the culture of their native hosts). Nor was that all. Along with her housewifely and motherly chores carried out under daunting physical conditions, she became proficient enough in the native language, and developed such friendly relations with its speakers, that they entrusted her with the recording and translation of scores of their never recorded folk tales — a remarkable achievement for someone without training in linguistics or anthropology. Needless to say, specialists in Solomon Island languages and cultures will welcome the rich new information contained in these folktales, but there is also much in them for anyone interested in the human condition anywhere and everywhere.

Douglas Oliver
Emeritus Professor of Anthropology
Harvard University

INTRODUCTION

Malaita is on the eastern side of the Solomon Island chain across from the more famous Guadalcanal. Approaching the island by air, it seems covered with an impenetrable green coat. Then, after landing at Auki, the capital, and traveling to the east side of the island by small boat following the shoreline, the heavy, dark, dense, overwhelming sense of the jungle intensifies. Mangrove trees grow down to the water's edge; there are few sand beaches. Arriving at the Lau Lagoon, the water is shallow with small islands containing houses inhabited by the Lau people. Additional houses are constructed on piles over the reef, and some low-lying artificial islands with more houses have also been created. These people rely on the abundant marine life, some coastal gardens, and trade with the hill people for their livelihood.

At the cove at the mouth of the Sasafa River is an entrance to Baegu territory. In the dense jungle of bushes and vines overshadowed by huge trees hundreds of feet tall, a network of narrow paths, known only to those who live there, leads to the interior. Exploring this area is not possible without a local guide. The narrow, muddy paths thread through sago palms, coconut palms, the gigantic canarium almond trees, bamboos and various hardwood trees as one hikes up the eastern side of the island. Blue-violet Borofunga mountain, often covered with misty white clouds, hovers overhead at about 3,200 feet. Climbing to higher elevations, the red slippery mud is left behind and the trails become mossy and rocky. Viewpoints are spectacular-the island seems to be suspended over the light blue reef below which is separated from the dark ocean by a line of white waves. At these higher elevations the climate is often misty and cool, especially at night.

The Sasafa River which runs through eastern Baegu territory is an incredible aqua blue and pure enough to drink. It flows swiftly between shallow rocky rapids and various deep pools surrounded by limestone cliffs. Each pool in the river has been given a name.

APPEARANCE OF THE PEOPLE

Malaitans are Melanesian. They are smaller than Caucasians; the average height of men being about five-feet-five inches and women about five feet. The people of the Lau Lagoon are larger and have well-developed upper bodies from years spent paddling canoes, while the Baegu hill people are leaner and more graceful from years spent walking on steep jungle paths. Though people in the western Solomons have deep blue-black skin, the people of Malaita have brown skin of varying shades. Children in the same family can range from light tawny to brown. Hair color is also variable, from reddish-blond, perhaps bleached by the sun, to brown or black. Most people have frizzy hair, but a few have straight black hair. Eyes are brown and facial structure is most often delicate.

There is an emphasis on breath or spirit. Lots of wind is needed to climb into the mountains, which the Baegu people do effortlessly in the jungle heat. They can project their voices for long distances when talking across jungle ridges and valleys, yet they can be so silent on densely wooded paths that no one can hear them. Singing can go on for hours, sometimes all night until the sun rises at 6 AM. Their wind instruments—the bamboo panpipes and the bamboo flute—also require lots of breath. Breath is equated with spirit, being thought of as an animating force. More breath means more life.

THE DAILY ROUTINE

The Baegu people rise at sunrise, which is about 6 AM all year long near the equator. A few cold taro or sweet potatoes left from the previous night's dinner provide breakfast. Adults go to their gardens from about nine in the morning to three or four in the afternoon. While mothers are in their gardens each day, young children are left with older children, other relatives, or sometimes their fathers. They are carefully cared for and are not usually allowed to crawl in the dirt and mud, but are carried until they can walk. Since they are constantly held and nurtured, they are usually happy and contented. Screaming, sobbing or whining are practically unknown.

Women spend more time than men in the gardens and return home in the afternoon with the day's supply of food plus huge bundles of firewood, seemingly too large for any person to carry.

Taro, sweet potatoes, the green vegetable *dee*, perhaps canarium almonds, coconut, or bananas create the evening's meal. The root vegetables are cooked in ovens in women's houses. These ovens are wood fires that heat rocks. The taro is placed over the rocks, covered with large moist leaves, then dry leaves. Dee is steamed in bamboo joints which are placed next to the fire. Drinking water is carried in bamboo joints with leaves carefully folded to create spouts on top of the bamboo sections.

Dinner cooks for an hour or so. Men are given their meals and eat separately. After dinner the adolescent boys of the village may sing while the rest of the village people watch. The boys usually quit after several hours, but sometimes when the moon is full they sing all night long.

All-night epic chanting *ae ni mae* done at memorial feasts honoring ancestors, is only for special occasions. Weddings also provide occasions for all night singing and story telling. At these times two rows of men sit facing each other and each man keeps time by clicking together two small sticks. At the head of the two lines sits the storyteller who chants the epic tales that follow.

How These Tales Were Collected

My anthropologist husband, our two older children (then seven and two years old, the third not yet born), and I were in Malaita for nearly four months before any folktales were told. It took time for us to get settled and resettled after a hurricane destroyed our house. And it took time for the people to become accustomed to us. Once they understood we were trying to get information about their culture, they were flattered yet apprehensive. It was just too strange, missionaries and government officials had not been interested in this kind of information. Malaita was poor, why were we doing this? They were suspicious. What was the real motive?

When we arrived no one in the village seemed fluent in English. A few men knew a limited amount of English, and the women knew none, so their language had to be learned. Once storytelling began, the men started with simple, short stories told in Baegu and worked up to the longer complicated ones. Women did not tell stories. I was there for one year and was not able to collect all the Baegu folktales. Unfriendly pagans farther up in the hills forbade some of the stories to be told, displeased that any were being told at all. Occasionally, these burly men would come and silently sit on our veranda and stare at us with menacing expressions.

Introduction

THE PEOPLE WHO TOLD THESE TALES

Most of these tales were told by men from Ailali, our village. Danny and Joel, both fairly fluent in English, were the two exceptions.

Basia was in his 40s and had been on Guadalcanal during World War II where he worked for the American army. An intelligent man, he had been taught to drive a truck while working for the army. A widower when we arrived, he surprised us by marrying one of the quiet, hard working widows in our village while we were there. An excellent musician, he played the Jew's harp, panpipes, and bamboo flute.

Meke, about 25 years old, had recently married one of the beauties of our village. Dark skinned, medium height with an athletic build, his eyes slanted slightly upward. He was energetic and always sought a leadership role. Though he was too young to be a village elder, it was obvious he intended to become one.

Lebefiu was a relatively small man with dark skin and a sprightly step. Interested in preserving the old customs of Malaita, he willingly modeled elegant, antique shell valuables so we could take his photograph. Probably in his fifties, he had four sons and a baby daughter. His oldest son, Matthew, was an invaluable help around our house. There was an aristocratic element to Lebefiu's personality, his posture was perfect and he seemed taller than he was. Though he spoke no English and had never spent time around Caucasians, he was one of the first people to understand and want to cooperate with what we were trying to do. Though he only helped tell one or two stories, he reserved the right to drop by frequently to see what progress was being made.

Danny was a good looking, pleasant man from Lau territory sent as a missionary by the Seventh Day Adventist Church to gain converts up in the hills. Coming from the Lau Lagoon, he was considered an outsider by the people who lived in and around our village. He only narrated one story, *Balairi*, which was one of the most intriguing. His English was quite good so translation problems were minimal.

Joel Rabelaisa was a slender, young, unmarried man, about 25, from a neighboring area who only came by occasionally. His English was excellent since he had spent years attending school. His family owned coconut groves near our village and when he came by he helped with thorny translation questions.

Micah Sedea, about 75, was one of the oldest men in the village. A relatively tall, lighter skinned man with white shining hair and a steady gaze, he was deferred to by others in the village because of his age and status. He had a tremendous memory and infinite patience. He spoke no English. Many months after he had begun telling stories, he mentioned he had been a houseboy in Tulagi, the capital of the British Solomon Island Protectorate before Honiara. "Missus Britisi," as he called her, had insisted he take baths, had put flowers on the dinner table, and had sailed off to Australia to rest. He had been married twice. His family had bought a light-skinned bride from a neighboring area for him when he was young. He had no children from this marriage. He then ran off with a second wife and had to pay her bride-price himself since his family didn't approve. He had no children from his second marriage either. Being without children he described himself sadly as being empty armed *aba gwaro*. His first wife had died, and the second was a very unassuming, agreeable woman of about 65.

Bauro, who usually accompanied Sedea, was a very quiet and gentle man with one leg amputated below the knee. Probably about 45, Bauro knew much more English than we first realized, having picked it up during lengthy hospital stays. With his injury he could not garden and was not married. He depended on others

Introduction

to provide food for him; there was something priestly and ascetic about him. He was willing to let us know how much English he knew only after the elders of the village decided stories would be translated. At first, he would answer most questions "I don't know," which could mean: "I don't understand the question"; "I don't know the answer to the question"; or "I don't want to answer the question." As time went on, he could answer almost all questions. He was a craftsman, making baskets from coconut palm fronds, carving clubs, and creating tortoise shell and abalone shell crosses.

Once Sedea decided he would tell folktales, there was no stopping him. He seemed to have a personal mission to tell as many as possible. Bauro was Sedea's ideal companion because of his quiet patience and knowledge of English. The two spent hours on the bench along the low wall of our veranda carefully telling stories while I wrote them down in Baegu and asked for translations of words and phrases I didn't understand. As I transcribed I could watch them as well as the panoramic view of Borofunga Mountain behind them.

I experimented with having Sedea use the tape recorder, but when I worked on translations he wasn't always there to answer questions. The narrative was also much more repetitive and lengthy than when I transcribed the stories directly, so I gave up the tape recorder. When talking to me Sedea made the tales more concise than they would have been when told at all-night singing sessions where time seemed endless and everyone relished intricate details.

I had not studied folklore before coming to Malaita. Perhaps one reason folktales were told was that Elli Köngäs Maranda, a folklorist, was collecting folktales among the Lau Lagoon people at the same time we were living among the Baegu people in the hills. This may have inspired the Baegu to tell their folktales. And

I discovered I enjoyed listening, so the tales were told. Elli and I saw each other occasionally and a few of the stories seemed similar. Many motifs found in folktales around the world — as catalogued in *Motif-Index of Folk Literature* by Stith Thompson — appear throughout these tales. **A few** of these motifs are listed with each tale.

While there I became a competent speaker of the language but did not understand all the nuances. (For example, I never tried to learn twelve different words describing betel nuts in various stages of ripening.) Given here are the stories, not with as much detail as they would have when told by a Baegu speaker to a Baegu audience, but with the plots and main characters intact.

MAPS

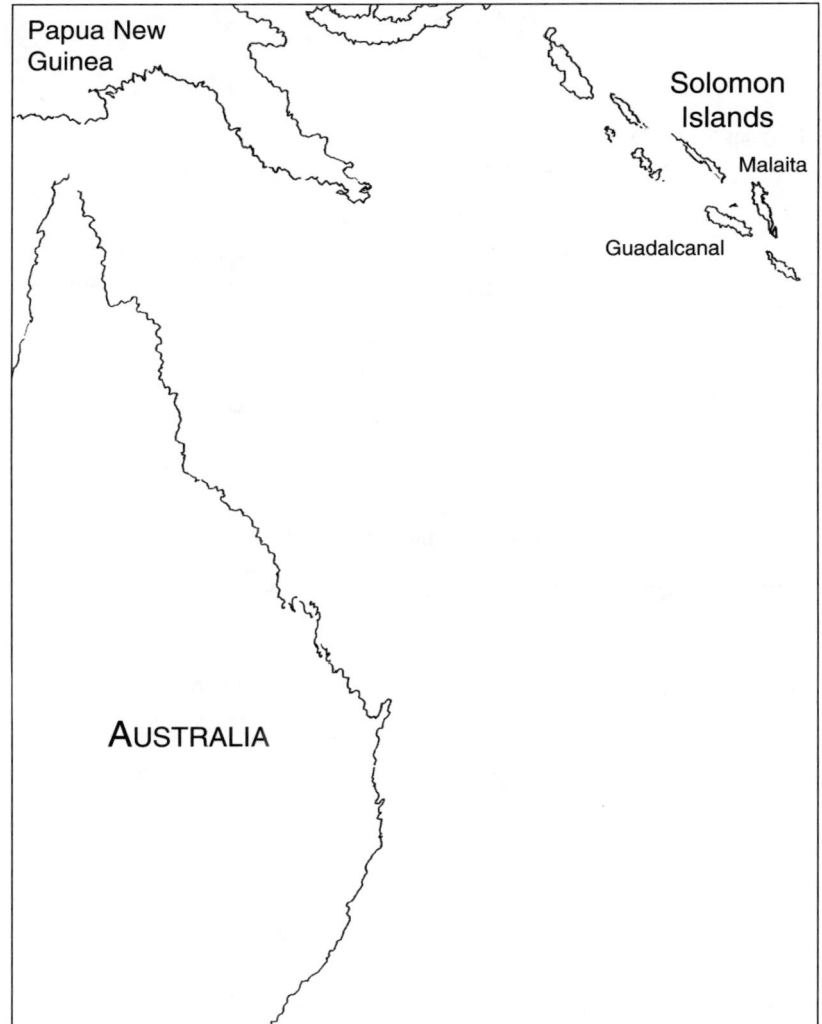

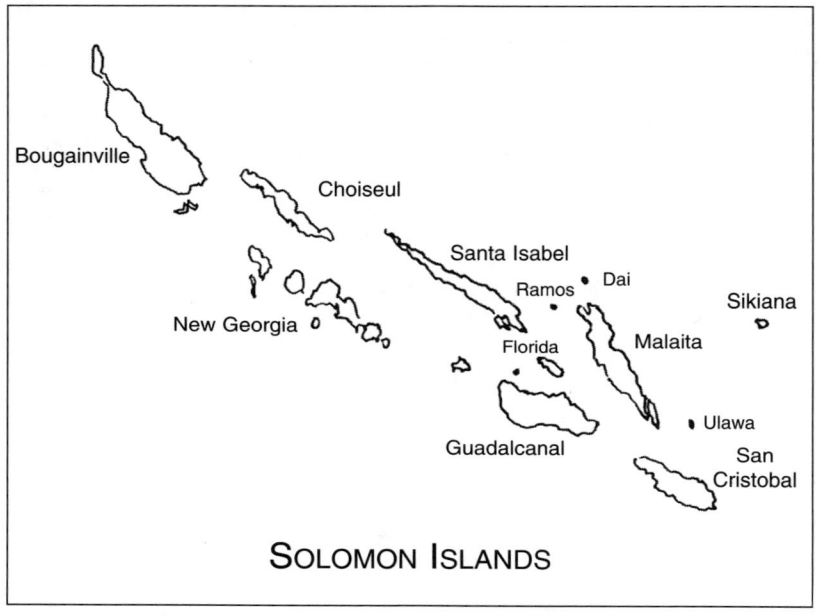

MAPS

Solomon Island Folktales from Malaita

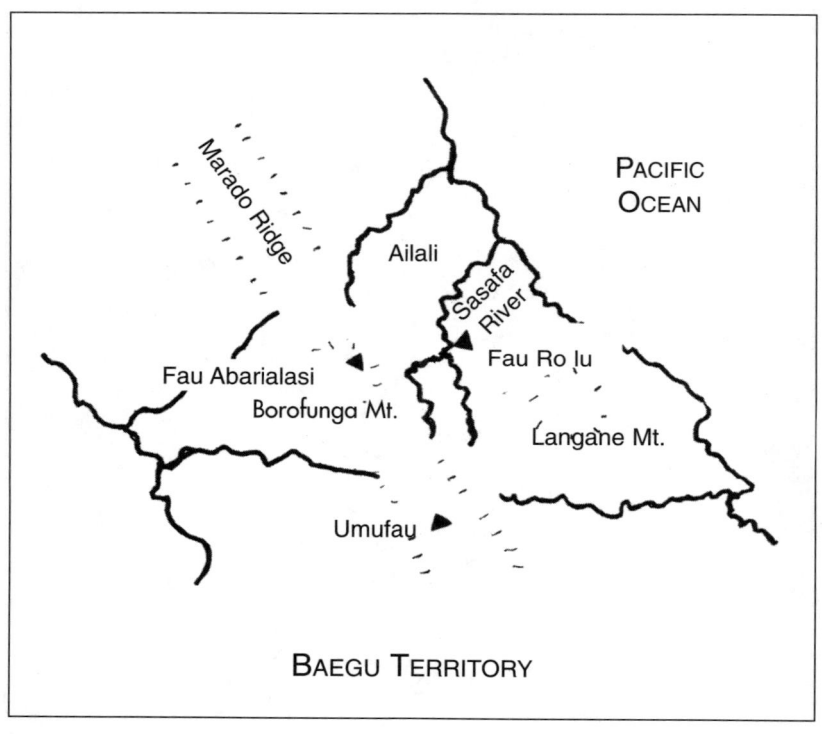

Photos

Ailali Village

Women at Market

MEN PERFORMING SACRED DANCE.

AILIKI AND LUIOMEA PLAYING BAMBOO PANPIPES.

Photos

Sasafa River: Lebefiu wearing shell necklace, Mathew third from left.

Boys with son Ted in a garden.

Solomon Island Folktales from Malaita

Two women returning from a pagan feast wearing porpoise teeth necklaces.

ORIGINS

THE BEGINNING OF BAEGU LANGUAGE — EXPLANATION
TOLD BY BAURO AND SEDEA, FEBRUARY 1967

A married couple living in Marado were the first to speak Baegu. The wife dreamed the new language one night and could no longer remember her previous language. She taught the new language to her husband and they both began speaking it. Their descendants continued speaking Baegu and founded eight ancestral clans. Marado is the Baegu ancestral homeland high on the mountain ridge above our village.

The wife was the creator of the new language and her husband followed her lead. Since women are so submissive in Baegu society this is surprising. Yet in the following story *Fire Rocks* a woman has a similar role.

Eight clans were formed. Eight was the preferred number, a special number frequently used in daily conversation and in folktales.

This tale may indicate that the Baegu language began on the top of Borofunga Mountain then later spread down to the eastern side of the island (where we were).

Baegu is not actually a separate language, but one of the five dialects found in Northern Malaita. In addition, there are also five other languages as one travels to the southern end of the island. Though called languages, they are not so different that people are totally unable to communicate since many people know other

Malaitan dialects and languages. Some Baegu folktales have characters that travel to other language areas *Two Sisters Bulifoia and Fulifoia* and on to other islands *Laenimota and Abarialasi, Niduramo*. Folktales also travel across Malaitan languages. For example, Ivens mentioned ideas found in southern Malaita that I recorded in the Baegu folktales *Canoe Building* and *House Building*.

Folktale Motifs: Origin of various clans
                          Dream as source of ideas

THE BEGINNING OF BAEGU LANGUAGE

A man named Nunu (Shadow) and his wife Fala (Giving) came from Marado. One night Fala dreamed of a new language, and when she awakened she could not remember her former language, she could only speak the language of her dream. She and her husband built a new village named Baegu where they both spoke the new language called Baegu. Their child Kabaesalo (Speaks from the Sky) also spoke this language, as did seven generations after him. Eight Baegu tribes were formed, and the language spread. Later Kaliau and his family brought the Baegu language to the Sasafa River and to Ataa, the eastern half of Baegu territory.

> Each of these men began a Baegu clan:
> Kabaesale lived at Anokefe
> Gagaulakwa lived at Gwaunaano
> Nui lived at Maanaano
> Rau lived at Takisalanwea
> Mamaea lived at Takisalabui
> Samaima lived at Anogwari
> Buria lived at Manakakalo
> Ramaoilalao lived at Uolalao

Origins

Fire Rocks and Fire Sticks — Explanation
Told by Sedea, Lebefiu, Bauro, and Meke, February 1967

These tales are also set in Marado. As in the previous story, woman's creative role is acknowledged is this Baegu myth where a young girl discovered the first fire when she saw fire in certain rocks. By striking together chert and iron pyrites she created sparks and started a fire.

Trying to start a fire without matches in a jungle with over 200 inches of rain a year is a challenge. Fires are carefully guarded, burning embers banked in ashes are always kept in the hearth, and fires are not allowed to go out.

The second fire started in Marado was begun by the brother of the girl who started the first fire. He noticed branches in a treetop rubbing together, climbed up, took these sticks home, and created a fire.

Starting a fire by rubbing a small stick in the groove of a larger stick with shavings of kindling nearby, was demonstrated for us by Lebefiu's son Matthew. This took skill, time and patience.

Fire Rocks

Everyone in Marado was digging up ground for a new house when they saw an unusual rock containing fire. One girl, Mamagu, took two of these rocks (iron pyrite and chert) home. She gathered small pieces of kindling, hit the two rocks sharply together, and the sparks lighted the kindling. The fire grew and made a lot of smoke. She cooked food and shared it with others. Everyone saw the fire and took home some of these rocks. From that time until today people have been cooking food with fires started with fire rocks.

Fire Sticks

When Gafurode, the brother of Mamagu, was walking along a path, he looked up and noticed the top branches of the tree rubbing together. He climbed to the top of the tree to watch the branches shaking, then he returned home with a branch. When he rubbed two pieces of the branch together, a fire lighted. A second fire was started in Marado.

ORIGINS

HOUSE BUILDING AND CANOE BUILDING — EXPLANATION
TOLD BY JOEL RABELAISA, FEBRUARY 1967

These brief stories give credit to magic talking animals who tell people how to build houses and canoes successfully. The idea of making notches in houseposts like the notched ears of a dog was recorded in southern Malaita by Ivens, (*Melanesians of the Southeast Solomon Islands*, 404). Also in this book, Ivens recorded the idea that the Masi were so foolish they caulked their canoes with mud, (410). As mentioned earlier, some stories are known throughout the island, despite the variety of dialects and languages.

Baegu people had little to do with canoes, since the Sasafa River was swift with shallow rapids between pools. However, the people of the Lau Lagoon used canoes, often dugout canoes, to constantly travel between the shore and islands in the reef. Lau children progressed through a series of canoes, each geared to their current size. From early experiences with small personal canoes, they gradually learned how to maneuver huge, heavy canoes throughout the reef.

Folktale motif: Animals assisting humans

HOUSE BUILDING

Two men from Arauma named Kunufia (Muddy Place) and Kakae (Cockatoo), and their relatives decided to build a bamboo house. They went into the forest to gather houseposts. They measured space for the house, dug holes for the posts, and dug two larger holes for the king posts. When these posts were firmly in place they tried to put the roof pole on top of the two king posts, but it slipped, fell, and killed twenty men. More men tried to lift it again, but the same thing happened. Next, eighty men came to work on the house. When half of them died trying to put up the roof pole, the remaining men heard a dog cry, "Look at my head!

Look at my head!" They looked at the dog's head and noticed the notch between his ears. So they cut notches in the king posts, put the roof pole in the notches, and found it was secure. From that time on, notches have been cut in king posts for bamboo houses.

CANOE BUILDING

Two men, Tagenao (Stand Fast) and Rifisao (Fish), talked about building a plank canoe tied with string. They cut boards of the right shape, made holes for the string, and tied the boards together. To make the canoe watertight, they closed the holes and cracks with earth, spreading a layer of the damp earth both inside and outside the canoe.

When they tried out the canoe in the sea, the mud washed off, and the canoe sank. They lifted it out of the water and carried it back to the hills where they had made it. Again they dug up earth to try to make the canoe watertight. While they were doing this a bird *fau* cried, "Sew it with string made from strong ferns *sata* then make it watertight with putty nuts *saie* and let it dry until it looks ashen." They followed these instructions and found that the canoe was watertight. From that time until today, plank canoes have been made this way.

WHY DEE HAS RED STEMS — EXPLANATION
TOLD BY MEKE, FEBRUARY 1967

This folktale explains why the common green leafy vegetable, which people eat every day, has red stems. Called *dee* (Hibiscus manihot) there actually were both red and white stemmed varieties.

The importance of offering the first fruits of a new garden to the priest cannot be overstated. Until the offering was given, no produce could be harvested. In pagan times it was a tabu not to be broken. In 1967, in our Christianized village, first fruits were still given, but to the church. The produce was then given to those unable to garden. For example, Bauro, who was an amputee, received baskets of taro which had been given to the church for first fruits offerings.

The cruelty to women seen in this story continues to be a common theme in these folktales.

WHY DEE HAS RED STEMS

Fauna, a woman from Marado, rose at dawn, picked up her gardening supplies, and went to her garden where she spent the day working. In the late afternoon when walking home, she saw a fallen log which was crushing some dee in her brother Mamaea's garden. She gathered some of the dee from under the log and put it in the crook of her arm, eager to return home and show it to him. The path passed in front of Mamaea's men's house where he was making a stone axe. Seeing her, he asked, "Fauna, where did you get that dee?"

She replied, "This is dee from your garden which a fallen log was crushing. Coming home I saw it, so I brought it with me."

Mamaea cried, "Who said you could bring back dee from my new garden? The first fruits have not been offered to the priest yet!" He was furious and hit Fauna on the wrist with the stone axe. Her blood began to flow over the bundle of dee she was carrying.

When Fauna took the dee from the garden the stems were white, but since her blood flowed over it, the stems have been red from that time to the present day.

ORIGINS

THE ORIGIN OF COCONUT, BETEL NUT, AND SAGO PALM — EXPLANATION
TOLD BY SEDEA AND BAURO, AUGUST 1967

According to this tale, these valuable palm trees — the coconut, betel nut, and sago (used for thatch to build houses) first appeared in Malaita growing from the corpse of a man. Obviously a foreigner, he was not buried in the traditional manner. Instead of being covered with mats and buried deep in the ground as was the Baegu custom, his body was thrown into a rocky pit.

When people saw the value of these plants, they enlisted the help of flying foxes to carry quantities of their nuts and seeds from other islands back to the high hills of Malaita. These seeds and nuts were taken to the village of Umufau (stone fire) a village high in the hills in neighboring Fatalaka territory.

In the Hawaiian language, *umu* is an archaic form of imu, which means oven, similar to the Baegu meaning. In the Baegu language umu is also an archaic word.

A flying fox also appeared in the tale *Sakwalofino*. In Baegu mythology, the flying fox seems to have the characteristics of being clever, magical and concerned with seeds and fertility.

Folktale motif: Plants growing from dead body.

THE ORIGIN OF COCONUT, BETEL NUT, AND SAGO PALM

Long ago a man called Walanifau (Shark Stone) had four homes, in Faibulue, Wawadake, Airirai (all not on Malaita), and Abaniasi (in Malaita) where his two sons Boregao and Bualigia lived.

When Walanifau was quite old he told his sons, "When I die I will give some valuable knowledge to both of you." The wise old man continued, "In fact, I will show something to the whole world."

Boregao questioned his father, "What knowledge are you going to show us?"

The father replied, "The two of you stay home with me until the time that I die, let my body rest for six days, then come back to see me." A short time later Walanifau died. Boregao carried his father's body to a rock graveyard where he dropped it into a hole in the sharp rocks. The brothers went back home to Abaniasi. After six days they returned to the rock hole where their father was lying. They saw a coconut sprouting from the top of his nose, a betel nut sprouting from one side of his mouth, and a sago palm budding from his testicles. The brothers said, "These are good things sprouting from the body of our father. This must be the knowledge he said he would give us."

The betel nut, the coconut, and the sago palm were just tiny budding plants, but they continued growing around the rock graveyard. When the coconuts and betel nuts were ripe, the brothers tasted them. They took these three plants to Abaniasi. They used the leaves from the sago palm to build houses.

Now the story turns to a man named Moekilu, who went to visit his friend Raonamelu from Malo. Raonamelu described the new plants he had seen growing in Abaniasi, the betel nut, the coconut, and the sago palm. Raonamelu and Moekilu decided that these plants should be known to everyone.

Moekilu returned to his home in Umufau and Daosaroe. He gathered two hundred flying foxes. They flew high up in the air, finally descending at Faibulue, Walanifau's first home.

There they saw the betel nut, coconut, and sago palm trees growing. The flying foxes broke the leaves and stalks of the trees while collecting their seeds and nuts. They flew with the nuts and seeds back to Umufau, where they were planted and grew well. From that time on, these plants have grown on Malaita.

ABUNAMALAU OR THE ORIGIN OF BANANAS AND SUGARCANE — EXPLANATION

TOLD BY SEDEA, JULY 1967

This folktale explains how bananas and sugarcane were introduced into Malaita with the help of the spirits living on the island of Dai, a small island north of Malaita reputed to be the dwelling place of the spirits. The bride, Abunamalau, was from Umufau, in the high hills of Fatalaka territory. Her husband was from Manu, which must be on the coast, because mangrove sticks were mentioned twice.

The marriage of Abunamalau and Alaiasi was rocky from the start and the birth of a child caused further tension and problems. Unhappy at home, Abunamalau seemed glad to be taken to the spirit world. Her first visit to Dai was a near death experience, and she did not seem sad when she later returned to Dai. She danced with the spirits in Dai, though Baegu women do not dance.

The two valuable plants—bananas and sugarcane—that she introduced to Malaita, are plants that are not to be eaten while in mourning according to the story *Black Magic*.

Besides being an origin myth, this tale has a secondary theme—the beating of women—which is a *leit motif* in Baegu folklore. Abunamalau was valued, the usual bride-price was paid for her, then a large reward was offered for her return. There is an implied warning here for husbands not to be cruel to valuable wives who provide so much labor.

Folktale motifs: Person sinking into the earth
Supernatural being punishes breach of tabu
Abundant food in otherworld
Spirits dwell on island
Revenant
Origin of cultivated plants

ABUNAMALAU OR ORIGIN OF BANANAS AND SUGARCANE

Barasao and two other men from the village of Manu (Bird) went looking for a wife to buy for Alaiasi, the son of Barasao. When they arrived at the village of Umufau (Stone Oven), located in the high hills of Fataleka territory, they called on Niu (Coconut) and asked about his daughter named Abunamalau (Blood in Hole in the Ground). Was she available to marry Alaiasi? Could they buy her? Niu replied that they could have her in exchange for ten strings of red shell money and one thousand porpoise teeth. Barasao agreed to this bride-price and explained that he was anxious to find a wife for his son so he would settle down and stay home.

So, the father, Barasao, returned to his village, Manu, gathered together the shell money and porpoise teeth, and took a large group of people with him back to Umufau. Arriving there, Niu told them to rest until daylight when they could lead the bride home.

The group gathered around the house of the bride-to-be and began the wedding tradition of all-night epic chanting. Two rows of men faced each other and kept time by the precise clicking together of two bamboo sticks while the chanter sat at the head of the two rows and sang folktales.

When day broke, they cut the bride's hair and placed red woven anklets on her legs and red woven bracelets on her wrists. She was led away to her new home in Manu. That night they also spread leaves in front of the house where she was staying and continued singing epic songs. In the morning it was the bride's task to pick up the leaves. While she was doing this, her father-in-law came by and thought she was very pleasing to watch.

The young couple lived in the same house for two months, but Abunamalau was too embarrassed to make love with her husband.

Origins

One day, Alaiasi's patience wore thin, and he angrily asked why she continued to refuse him. She answered, "If only you had not asked me with so many people around."

Her husband replied, "Why do you forbid yourself since I have paid for you with my family's money?" She only responded, "We have many days ahead of us yet." Alaiasi and Abunamalau remained cool and distant.

Barasao was also angry when he heard about this argument. He picked up a knotted mangrove stick and threw it at his daughter-in-law. The stick hit the back of her leg, and blood began to flow. She was furious and cried, "My father has forbidden you to take blood from me." She fled and lived alone in the forest until she was about to die.

At this time, Kwadibulu, a spirit from the island of Dai, left his island and came to the place where she was hiding. He picked up lime dust, threw it on her, then carried her off to Dai. Arriving there at dusk, and leading her by the hand, he placed her in the center of a group of spirits who were dancing the traditional dance honoring ancestors, the *wai*. She joined them. The heads of the spirit people wobbled back and forth as they danced. But hers did not wobble even though she danced as they did, because she was alive, and her head was firmly attached. The spirits noticing the living girl added to their group were surprised and delighted. They laughed and shouted around her.

Two men nearby, Fauabu (hawk) and Naoabu (eagle) heard all this laughing and shouting which continued for many days. They wondered, "What is this noise? What are the spirits laughing and shouting about over there?" They went, stood silently watching the dancing, and noticed the girl whose head was not shaking.

Naoabu said, "There is Abunamalau, daughter-in-law of Barasao from Manu, dancing with the spirits. Her husband and father-in-law are searching for her. Let's carry her back to Manu because there is a reward of one hundred pieces of shell money and porpoise teeth for her return."

Careful preparations were made. The two of them smeared their bodies with lime dust and ginger. They also ate some ginger and held pieces of it in their mouths. Arriving quickly at the dance ground, they leapt into the center of the group, snatched Abunamalau, and fled with her. The leader of the spirits, Kwadibulu, chased after them crying, "You two come back with my woman. You must not take her."

Then reconsidering the situation, he called, "Wait, wait until I give some of our bananas and sugarcane to Abunamalau. She needs to plant them in her garden so she will have good food to help her regain her breath (strength) since she is weak from dancing for days with the spirits. Take her back to her husband. This time he must look after her well, because if another time she should come back to Dai, she will not leave."

The two men put her into a canoe along with the bananas and sugarcane and paddled to Manu where they collected the prize money from Barasao for returning Abunamalau. When she was again with her husband Alaiasi, she told him, "We will live happily together, but only as long as you do not get angry with me; because if you scold or punish me, I shall die."

Bananas and sugarcane were planted in their garden, and they lived contentedly together until Abunamalau became pregnant and gave birth to a child. They fed it carefully and it grew fat with the help of the new foods they had planted.

Then one day Abunamalau told her husband, "You stay home and look after our child while I go to the garden to bring home some food." So Alaiasi carried the child about, but it cried. The more he tried to soothe it, the more it screamed. He thought, "Today when my wife comes back I'm going to beat her for telling me to stay home with this child which has done nothing but cry since she left."

Abunamalau returned home and threw her heavy bundle of food down in front of the house. Her husband, holding the child in his left hand, stood up and kicked Abunamalau and shouted, "Why have you stayed in the garden so late? This baby has done nothing but scream all day long!"

His wife stood very still and cried bitter tears. "You have done that which is forbidden, you must not hit me."

Alaiasi held up the baby and said, "Take the child; suckle it." But she did not tend to her child and stood silently crying. Her legs began to sink into the ground up to her knees. Alaiasi ordered, "Stop your crying. Take care of the child. Let it nurse!" But by this time she had sunk down to her waist. As the ground reached her neck, she said, "You must take good care of our child." Her husband took a knotted mangrove stick and quickly dug up the ground around her. But only her voice came back and repeated her plea, "You must take good care of our child."

He kept trying to dig up the ground around her, but all he heard was her voice. "You must take good care of your child. I am leaving you now, I am returning to Dai. I shall dance with the spirits there."

THE ORIGIN OF TARO — EXPLANATION

TOLD BY MEKE AND JOEL REBELAISA, FEBRUARY 1967

Two men Sinakwao (white hair) and Aokwao (white panpipes) discovered taro growing in a rock outcropping. The name of this taro was Fau i Marado (rock in Marado).

The Malaitan interest and emphasis on gardening appears in this tale. The careful cultivation of taro plants, then when they are ripe, the careful planting of taro tops to ensure the next crop is described. Taro is a favorite food, preferred over sweet potatoes. Pork is the ultimate treat, enjoyed only on special occasions. Another theme is the first fruit offering, this time an elaborate ceremony involving the preparation of many sacrificial pigs.

The white imagery in the names of the discoverers of taro echoes the type of taro grown in Marado. Taro from the high hills in Marado is gray-white and peppery in taste while taro from gardens by the coast is reddish and bland. This is caused by the type of soil in which the plant is grown.

Ivens reported that a rock sculpture in the shape of a pig was located on Marado ridge. (*Island Builders of the Pacific*, 286.) I did not see or hear about this sculpture.

Folktale motifs: Transformation: pig changed into a rock
taro called rock

ORIGIN OF TARO

Two men discovered a taro plant. Their names were Sinakwao (White Hair) and Aokwao (White Panpipes). The name of the taro was Fau i Marado (Rock in Marado). This taro plant grew in the middle of a rock outcrop. They fenced in the taro and fertilized it by putting ashes around the stems. The taro grew large. When the day for harvesting arrived, the woman Kwaoalafa (In Love with White Hair) dug up the taro. The two men took digging sticks and prepared the ground for a garden, then planted the taro tops. The taro grew well and when it was ready to harvest, it was time for a first fruit offering. A feast was planned, and forty pigs were fattened. The priest Subia also brought another forty pigs to this feast which took place in Marado. They gave out taro to everyone there to take home and plant in their gardens.

The pigs for the feast were brought in one by one. The first was called Fulungangara (Hanging Tree Roots). The next one was named Bosoaabu (Red Pig). Then came Meroabula (Bloody Ass). They began to prepare them for the feast. When they were working on the pig Meroabula a strange thing happened. After singeing the hair, they began scraping the skin, and while scraping its midsection, a priest said, "Suppose this pig runs away?" No sooner were the words spoken than the pig got up and fled. It ran quickly, but soon fell to the ground where its body was changed into a stone, Fau i Marado (Rock in Marado).

FOOLS

TALES ABOUT FOOLS — EXPLANATION

These tales featuring fools take place in Marado, the ancestral homeland. The first four stories are concerned with the production, collection, preparation or consumption of food. They depend on the double meaning of a word for their humor. The poor fools *wane oewanea* listen to instructions from thinking men *wane manata* then misinterpret the message and do the wrong thing, often for hours.

Common everyday settings are the background for these tales. In the story about making soup, most people go to their gardens during the day leaving only a few adults or older children to look after younger children. So Kwaoa taking care of a group of children during the day would be the normal routine.

In the story about almond trees, climbing canarium almond trees was a specialty of the men from the hills. Their agile strength and sense of balance were necessary for climbing these huge trees. Men from the seacoast hired hill men to climb their almond trees since they were afraid to do it themselves. The fool in this story was at least smart enough to know how to climb the tree, he just didn't know what to do when he got there.

In the story about black ants, eating insects was not unusual. When caches of certain bugs were found when overturning logs or rocks, they were quickly devoured, providing a change of diet from the ever-present sweet potatoes and taro.

The fifth story is concerned with the strict sexual tabus of the Baegu.

These stories provide comic relief as well as examples of what not to do. Ivens thinks stories about the foolish people of Marado relate to the stories about the Masi, silly little people found in southern Malaita, (Ivens, Walter G., *Island Builders of the Pacific, 1930,* 286). The Masi are also mentioned in connection with the final folktale *The Pig Beukwalangia*.

Folktale motif: Fools

Four Tales about Fools
Told by Meke, February 1967

Kweoa was a fool. One day the smart people of Marado who were all going to their gardens told him, "Since you are staying in the village with the children, at noon make a soup to warm up their chests *ako i ruruna*." So he cooked soup, and when it was ready he told all the children to lie down. Then he stood over them and spilled some soup on the chest of each child, burning the chests of all the children.

ako i ruruna means:
1. warm chest, similar to warm stomach
2. burn chest

Maea was a fool from Marado. One day the smart people of Marado said to him, "Today you must finish building that fence *labua sakali* which is incomplete" So he went to the garden where the fence was not finished and stood there throwing logs at the end of the unfinished fence from morning until night. Then he went home and said he had done what they asked until nightfall.

labua means to strike or hit

labua sakali means to build a fence

Fools

Magai was a fool from Marado. One day his wife said to him, "Go climb that canarium almond tree, take some rope to climb it, and harvest *kwaia* the nuts." So he went to the tree, wrapped some rope around his ankles and cut another rope to help him climb the tree. Then he began cutting slashes in the trunk of the almond tree working his way up to where the branches began. Returning home he announced, "I've finished *kwaia* that almond tree." His wife was surprised because she didn't see any almonds.

kwaia means:
   1. to hit or slash
   2. to cut fruit or nuts as when harvesting

Manualili was a fool from Marado. One day the smart people of Marado told him, "Light a fire *suangia* to burn the huge black ants in the garden." So he went to the garden and lit a fire. He held one of the ants to the fire, cooked it, and ate it. Then he did the same with one hundred more ants. The following morning he continued to cook and eat ants.

suangia means:
   1. light a cooking fire (for eating)
   2. light a fire (for getting rid of, to burn and destroy)

Mamaea, a Gullible Fool — Explanation
Told by Meke, February 1967

Mamaea, a man from Marado returns to the men's house after making love to his wife and asks for help in curing the fiery sore between her legs. Sakwalofino offers to help cure the sore, but his treatment makes Mamaea so angry a fighting party is gathered to attempt to kill him. However, Sakwalofino escapes by changing into a flying fox.

Mamaea is also mentioned in the tale *Origin of Baegu Language* as the founder of one Baegu clan. This name also appears in *Why Dee Has Red Stems*.

The transformation to a flying fox is interesting. In another tale, *The Origin of Coconut, Betel Nut and Sago Palm* flying foxes are used to carry new seedlings to Malaita. However, in this tale the flying fox brings a different type of seed (sperm).

A recurring theme found again in this tale is that adultery is punishable by death.

Folklore motifs: Gullible fool
Transformation from man to animal

Mamaea, A Gullible Fool

Mamaea, a man from Marado, after making love to his wife Sigaabula, came back to the men's house and said, "One of you come help me find a cure for my wife's fiery sore between her legs." One of the men there, Sakwalofino, said, "I know how to cure these things. We'll go get medicine." So Mamaea and Sakwalofino went to Mamaea's home in Malume, where Sakwalofino said, "Shut the door. Sigaabula and I will stay in the house." Mamaea closed the door and left. Then Sakwalofino committed adultery with Mamaea's wife during the day. Everyone in the village noticed and told Mamaea when he returned. He was furious, but by the time he reached his house, Sakwalofino had fled.

Mamaea gathered together a fighting party to kill Sakwalofino. After a long chase they finally caught him. Sakwalofino said, "Take me and throw me off a high cliff." They carried him to a cliff and threw him off. He fell, but before reaching the ground, he began flying away as he had changed into a *sakwalo* or flying fox.

WOMEN

The next group of folktales describe the various ways women adapt to this culture. Baegu women do what is expected of them, otherwise they seem to commit suicide, or run away from home. Another group of women not from Malaita, have special powers, as will be seen in two of these tales.

WHY WOMEN ARE TABU — EXPLANATION
TOLD BY MEKE, SEDEA AND LEBEFIU, MARCH 1967

This tale describes the sexual Puritanism prevalent among the Baegu. Married women are not flirted with nor do they flirt. Women do not dance. If they sing it is in small groups among themselves. Occasionally women play the flute but not panpipes or drums. Young girls make amazing drum-like sounds by beating water in the river with their bare hands.

Pagan Malaitans believe that menstrual blood and childbirth are very contaminating to men. Women must separate themselves going to special huts during periods. At the time of childbirth they go alone to a remote hut to have their child. One friend or relative brings food while the mother and baby remain there a month before returning to the village.

To marry, a young man must buy a wife with from five to ten pieces of red shell money *tafuli'ae*. These impressive shell valuables each consist of ten strands of red shell discs six feet long.

Brides must be hard working since their cost is high. Women

do most of the gardening and carry their huge loads of firewood and garden produce over steep and difficult terrain. Men carry clubs or spears. Their hands must be free in case of warfare is the rational for carrying no burdens.

Women do not object to being paid for, in fact they are proud of their worth and how much bride-price they attract. The marriage contract is taken very seriously.

This story points out the problems of taking a woman without properly marrying her. Fury, murder, and curses follow.

Folktale motif: No wars because of women

WHY WOMEN ARE TABU

It is the custom among the Baegu that no man may make advances to a married woman. If a strange man enters the bedroom of a married woman or steps over her bundles or mats and commits adultery with her, he can be killed by her husband or children. The custom began with the story of Kariomae.

A girl, Kariomae, came alone to 'Ore'Ore from Bora and was found by Ramoidaafi, who took care of her. One day they went to the market in Kwara'Ae where her beauty was noticed by Kuluabu. He abducted her and carried her up to the hills of Marado where they lived together. Ramoidaafi, furious, cursed the villages up in Marado.

Later Kuluabu went to the market at Aenabubulo where he met his friend Bulao who told him, "My friend, this is a terrible thing you have done, stealing Kariomae. Ramoidaafi's testicles are furious. He has cursed Marado with the powerful curses of *Basi* (bow), *Mana Ramoe* (Fighting Men's Curse) and *Mana Aba Filu* (Curse of the Red Palm Leaves) because Kariomae has stayed with you in her new home in Marado without being married."

After hearing this, Kuluabu returned to his home in Marado and gathered together a fighting party to go to 'Ore'Ore and kill Ramoidaafi for cursing him. Arriving there they killed Baa, a relative of Ramoidaafi, in place of Ramoidaafi. By doing this they purged their homestead in Marado of the curses put on it by Ramoidaafi.

When they returned home they raised a huge shout, pounded the drums, and blew the triton's trumpet to celebrate their success. They offered pigs and prayed to the ancestral spirit *akalo* and wore fern leaves in their hair.

Because a man was killed due to an argument over a woman, all the most powerful curses may be invoked to prevent anyone from stealing a woman. These curses are called *Basi* (bow), *Mana Ramoe* (fighting Men's Curse), and *Mana Aba Filu* (Curse of the Red Palm Leaves), and have been used from that time until today.

Two Wives — Explanation

Told by Sedea, July 1967

Edikau makes the mistake of accepting a valuable necklace from one man then marrying someone else. Her first suitor uses magic to cause her illness since he feels angry and betrayed. When her husband brings in another wife, actually a former girlfriend, Edikau is so angry she commits suicide.

This folktale points out the fact that a woman should not accept presents from one man then marry another. Talking to strange men and even talking to men at all is frowned upon and not done by virtuous young girls.

This tale makes it obvious that two wives can cause problems for men, though among pagans it was not forbidden if the man could afford it.

When the mother-in-law found Edikau dead, she seemed more upset about the loss of bride-price than the loss of her daughter-in-law.

A recurring Baegu theme is the drawing of black lines on each side of the mouth when the mind is no longer able to think clearly and insanity approaches.

Folktale motifs: Disease caused by magic
                      Disease cured by magic

Two Wives

A young man, Kafaikau, had been looking around for a bride in the village of Mota. One day he saw a pretty girl he didn't know working in a garden and decided to watch her more closely. Her name was Edekau, and her father had brought her up strictly not allowing her to speak to strangers. Kafaikau carved designs on the surface of a betel nut and threw it at her. The betel nut landed on her breast and hurt her. She couldn't see who had thrown it, but later standing silently by a fence, she saw

Kafaikau. They talked for a while in a secret place hidden by trees. Kafaikau took off a porpoise tooth necklace and gave it to Edekau, saying he would come back and buy her as his wife. He told her not to talk to any other strangers.

Meanwhile, the relatives of another young man, Maboilau, were looking for a wife for him. Seeing Edekau at a market, they asked her relatives about buying her. Her father was agreeable; and Edekau, wanting to see what Maboilau looked like, met him at the market where they exchanged presents of taro and fish. They chewed betel nut together and agreed to marry.

After many preparations, on the agreed-upon day, the groom's family arrived at the bride's home bringing one hundred strings of shell money and two thousand porpoise teeth. Maboilau's mother led her new daughter-in-law home with her, and as her companion came a child, little Edekau, her namesake. The marriage festivities lasted several days with singing continuing all through the night.

Not long after the wedding, Kafaikau, who had been away to other areas of the island returned home. Finding his younger brothers sleeping, he kicked them to wake them up and find out where they had been to make them so tired. They told him about Edekau's marriage, and he was furious. Then he wept, fell into bed and refused to eat, drink, or bathe. He could think of nothing but Edekau. His sister tried to talk him into finding another girl, but he remained alone and grieved for another month. Then he took some shell money and went to a faraway place named Fauiwane to buy a magic power to poison the woman who had betrayed him.

Arriving in Fauiwane he explained to Bari, a man who dealt in magic, what he wanted. Before daybreak the next morning in a sacred grove of trees, Bari spoke to a certain plant. He explained to the plant what was wanted and told it if it was not willing to be used this way it should keep all its leaves. However, the leaves fell down. These leaves were put in a bamboo container, crushed with a stick, and covered with a tight lid. Kafaikau was instructed not to drink, urinate, or spit. He must stay tabu with the plant, or he would again lust after Edekau and the poison would not work.

He found Edekau and her husband working in their garden. He hid upstream from a watering place where she would probably come for a drink. He spoke to the plant, telling it who he wanted killed, exhorting it to use its power. He hid above the spouting water behind foliage. Edikau became thirsty and went for a drink. He held his magic leaf above the spout. Edekau drank deeply.

Not long after returning to the garden, she fainted. Her husband Maboilau begged the ancestral spirit in Kafoere to give her back her breath (health). They slowly walked back to their village. When everyone there saw how ill the bride that cost one hundred shell strings of money looked, they were very concerned.

Edekau was sick for months and grew very thin. She was near death and unable to talk. Her husband sent his relatives to find a remedy for the evil magic attacking his wife. Pigs and porpoise teeth were promised to anyone who could make her well. Maboilau built an isolated shelter for the two of them to live in together. His older brother told him to stay there until Edekau was dead.

Abaae from Takwa came to see if he could cure her, but Maboilau did not want anyone to see his wife. Edekau suddenly became conscious, as though with the consciousness that comes just before death. Maboilau decided to let Abaae see his sick wife. When Abaae lifted the mat covering her face, he immediately recognized what magic was killing her, magic from Fauiwane. He directed Maboilau to bring back many leaves of the blue cordyline plant in a bamboo section filled with water. Abaae took these leaves and chewed some ginger and betel nut. Maboilau took the mat from Edekau's body. Abaae spit the ginger from his mouth all over her, then taking the bamboo section he poured the water with blue cordyline leaves into her mouth. He listened to the water running inside her chest. Finally he tied some of the leaves around her neck. Then he left with the arrangement that if he did not hear the drum call announcing her death, he would return in six days.

As soon as Abaae had left, Edekau asked her husband for a bit of food. Perspiration covered her face. Later she ate taro and fish which her husband prepared for her. She regained her strength and six days later her husband gave ten strings of shell money, one thousand porpoise teeth, and ten pigs to Abaae for bringing his wife back to life. Accepting his presents, Abaae told Maboilau, "From now on you must look after your wife carefully." Before leaving he cut off the cordyline leaves he had tied around Edekau's neck. When Edekau had regained all the weight she had lost, the couple returned to their house in the village where everyone came to see them.

When Edekau felt stronger, she suggested that she and her husband go work in the garden. But Maboilau kept delaying. He talked to his mother, saying he was afraid to go to the garden. Someone might kill him with evil magic. Instead of gardening, he asked his mother to arrange for the family to buy him another wife so the two wives could garden together without him. He asked for Alinaoe to be chosen as his second wife, since she was a former girlfriend he had known before he met Edekau. Little Edekau overheard this conversation without being noticed. She was afraid to tell Edekau who was staying in the menstrual hut what she had overheard. When she did, Edekau was dismayed.

Edekau was working in the garden on the day she knew the other bride was coming to live with them. Late that afternoon when Edekau knew the bride would be there, she returned home with a huge bundle of five hundred taro and firewood which she threw down in front of the house with such force that the ropes broke. This noise frightened eighty pigs which got loose and ran away. She glared at the new bride, "Who is that?" Her mother-in-law explained to her that Alinaoe had come so she would have help with all of her work. Edekau cursed the new bride and Alinaoe cursed back. Suddenly with fury Edekau picked up a digging stick and struck her rival in the head. Blood flowed. "You came to commit adultery!" she screamed at the new bride. "You tricked me," she accused her husband, "you had already taken a wife before you married me."

After this scene she left with little Edekau to stay in the women's menstrual hut. Unseen magic powers took away her reason. During the middle of the night while her namesake slept, she put on a porpoise teeth necklace her father had given her as well as all of her other valuables. She drew black lines on each side of her mouth. Then she tied an intricate series of knots, making a noose for herself. She bid farewell to her husband and his new wife and hung herself.

Her mother-in-law was the first to discover her body. She cried out awakening the family, "The wife we bought with one hundred strings of red shell money is dead! She has killed herself because Maboilau married another woman."

WOMEN

A SPECIAL TREE — KAKALA AE — EXPLANATION
TOLD BY MEKE, JUNE 1967

This decorated tree did not have spiritual meaning or ties to the ancestors, it was a personal statement of wealth and property.

The owner of this tree announced cruel treatment would result from anyone who broke the tree, any man would be killed, any woman would suffer from fire. By lying, the woman who broke the tree managed to shift the blame to another woman. The wrongly accused is injured and commits suicide. Cruelty to women is a recurring theme in these stories and suicide is a way out when a Malaitan woman can bear no more.

The women in this tale do not work together to prevent cruelty, one turns on the other to save her own skin.

This was the first mention of Abarialasi rock. Questions about the rock led to the telling of the *Laenimota and Abarialasi* a love story recorded later.

Folktale motifs: Innocent made to appear guilty
Treacherous relative

A SPECIAL TREE — KAKALA AE

Near the famous rock called Abarialasi, Basiaro prepared for himself a special tree called a *Kakala Ae*. He trimmed the lower branches and formed the top branches into a top knot. Then he decorated the tree with strings of porpoise teeth and shell valuables. He finished by putting a long torch and a lighted spear in the trunk. Then he vowed, "If any man breaks down my tree I will kill him with this spear. If any woman breaks it I will burn her with this torch." The fame of the tree spread, and Basiaro constantly watched over it.

Meanwhile Basiaro's nephew Mamaoa, who lived in Fau Baite with Basiaro, was building a new house in nearby Fau Niu.

He planned a housewarming party for his new home and went to the offshore island of Funaafou to ask for one thousand fish for the celebration. His brothers asked for one thousand taro from the gardens high in the hills in Anobobosu. A group of girls carrying these taro for the feast walked along the path by the decorated tree. Edaikao, ahead of the group, was the first to see the tree. While playing with the unusual tree, she accidentally broke the trunk, but then cleverly set it upright again so that it did not appear to be broken. When one of the other girls, Maomekona, who was Mamaoa's sister, came by with a huge bundle of taro on her back, she accidentally brushed against the tree, and it fell over. The other girls screamed, "You broke the Kakala Ae. Now we're in trouble." "It wasn't me," she insisted, "I didn't hear the tree crack. Someone else broke it!" They ran home terrified by what had happened.

Basiaro found his broken tree and stood by it asking all who came by if they knew who had done the damage. When Edaikao walked by she said, "My cousin Maomekona broke it with the edge of the pack on her back."

That evening Basiaro and his brothers took lighted torches and began the search for Maomekona. They found her alone in her home. First Basiaro asked her for some food. She gave him some cold fish and taro. Then the men lighted a torch and began burning her body, singeing off all the hair on her body, beginning with her underarms until they bled and continuing on to her pubic hair. Finally they burned all the hair on her head.

Bleeding, ashamed, and afraid she hid from everyone. Later when no one was in the house, she braced the door shut with a stick, then took the rope from her pack, tied it on a cross beam, made knots in it, and hung herself.

BALAIRI — EXPLANATION

TOLD BY DANNY, MEKE AND SEDEA, JULY 1967

In Malaitan pagan culture the low status of women makes it impossible for the young girl Balairi to witness sacred rituals. When she does, she defiles sacred priestly prayers and they must be changed. Because of the priest's wrath she commits suicide, but is saved from death by life-giving waters from a tree root. The concept of life-giving waters from tree roots also appears in two other stories, *Warrior Women* and *Two Sisters Builfoia and Fulifoia*.

Going by underground stream to the sea, she encounters and lives with a man knowing the magical powers of the sea gods. From this union she gives birth to two eggs. From each egg a child emerges and these twins grow up to kill their father, eat him, and escape into the forest.

The twins killing their father from the sea annul the powers of the sea gods. Then the twins return to the forest, their mother's home. The tension between the forces of the hill and sea people reflected in this story reinforces the fear and separation that exist between the mountain and coastal peoples.

There is an absolutely beautiful place, a deep pool surrounded by rock cliffs in the Sasafa River, called *Fau Ro Iu* which means twin rock. Drinking the water which comes cascading down the sheer cliff sides into the pool is said to cause twins. This area is farther up the river than we usually went and the people did not seem to approve of us being there. This pool is also mentioned in the folktale *Black Magic*.

There were no living sets of twins that we met in Malaita. Though we knew of three people who had been born as twins, in each case the other twin had died in infancy.

Folktale motifs: Birth from an egg
Underground passage

SOLOMON ISLAND FOLKTALES FROM MALAITA

Twins

Children killing father

BALAIRI

Balairi's mother, Taeasalo, went to visit her brother-in-law, Abunilonga, who was a priest. She said, "If you will give a feast and sacrifice a pig on behalf of our hamlet of Gwaunafilu, I will give you a choice pig that has lain around so long that his tusks have grown curved into complete circles. It will be yours, if you give the feast." Abunilonga replied, "Good, I will do it."

Abunilonga left Gwaunafilu to look for taro leaves. He brought back many of these and also picked up the special pig to be sacrificed. Then he warned people, "Come daylight, every man and woman in Anogwari (including Gwaunafilu) must stay indoors. I will be doing sacred things, and women must not watch a priest at work."

He slept but got up early and went to the place of sacrifice at Tofuanga before daybreak. He sacrificed the pig by binding its snout with a fiber cord and holding it by its legs over his shoulder, praying to the gods of Gwaunafilu, while the pig died of strangulation. Laying the carcass by the taro leaves, he went to work with his stone adze to cut firewood to cook the pig. He first singed the pig over a hot fire, then by mid-morning, after the fire had burned down, he roasted the pig in a stone and leaf oven. Then he cut up the pork and divided it into proper portions.

Meanwhile, Balairi thought to herself, "Even though my uncle forbade it today, I will go to the sacred grove and look at what he does there as a priest, because in days to come I will marry, live in my husband's hamlet, bear his children, and be far away from here." So Balairi went through the forest to the gate through the stone wall around the place of sacrifice, and quietly watched Abunilonga while he sacrificed, cooked, and cut up the pig.

Women

As the sun rose, it cast Balairi's shadow which moved over the stone wall and magically floated around the sacrifice area. Abunilonga looked up, saw the shadow, spun around and saw Balairi. He realized Balairi had seen and heard the sacred ritual. He stood up, dropped the pig, and shouted, "Balairi, you have done a terrible thing. You have defiled a sacred place!"

Balairi, terrified, fled back to her house. At noontime, Abunilonga returned to Gwaunafilu and told her, "You have defiled a sacred place, you must go away from here forever. The men of Gwaunafilu, of Marado, and Mangoana are so angry that their testicles burn because of this sacrilege." Since Balairi had ruined the sacred prayers, they were immediately replaced with new ones.

Balairi listened and wept bitterly. She was very despondent. In despair, she stood on a bench, took a coil of rope, and tied one end to a roof beam. Pulling it tight, she made a noose in the other end. She rose, took a betel nut and placed it between her lips, and stood there tautly. Standing on the bench, she put the noose around her neck, drew up her legs and hung herself.

Her mother, Taeasalo, came home, opened the door, saw her daughter hanging there, and screamed. For her funeral Balairi's body was covered with pandanus mats and carried out to be buried. In the past, pandanus mats were not tightly sewed around the head of the dead as they are today. They lowered her into her grave.

As she lay in the grave, a tree root twisted around her and burst. Life giving water from the root flooded into the mat shroud covering Balairi and filled the shroud like a ripening fruit. The water flowed into her mouth, ran into her stomach, and brought her to life again. She got out of the shroud and traveled through an underground fissure until she came to a large subterranean river. She rode along with the current, following the river until she arrived at the sea.

A man named Uuta saw Balairi, but he was afraid of her because one of her hands always stayed on her lips. Balairi floated until she came to rest on an island. Uuta picked her up, brewed a potion having the magical power of the sea gods, and made her drink it. At once her hand fell away from her lips.

Balairi lived with Uuta as his wife. They lived together until Balairi became pregnant. She was pregnant for a year, then gave birth to two eggs that fell to the ground and broke. From one broken egg came a boy child, from the other a girl child. Later these two egg-children fashioned weapons of stone, went to the house of Uuta, their father, killed him and ate him. When they had finished this, they escaped into the forest.

WOMEN

WARRIOR WOMEN AND GHOSTS — EXPLANATION

TOLD BY SEDEA AND MEKE, JUNE 1967

This is a tale of power and introduces a new type of woman who is totally different from the women who commit suicide in the previous stories.

There are four types of "people" in this story: Malaitan men, Malaitan women, ghosts, and warrior women.

The Malaitan men lose their wives when they are abducted by evil ghosts. Two men of a large group of Malaitan men searching for the evil ghosts are killed by the ghosts while the other men are powerless to save them.

The Malaitan women captured by the ghosts manage to exist with the ghosts on a rock in the sea. They refuse to become their lovers and they refuse to eat raw human meat, the ghosts' regular diet. The ghosts make an unusual suggestion to them-in order to prevent their being caught by other evil ghosts, if they each would allow their blood to be drained from a cut in the arch of a foot, they would be invisible and able to fly. The women agree to this, their heavy blood flows out of their bodies and they can fly. But then the ghosts order them to stay in the house.

The ghosts *gosile* are feared because of their cannibalism, superhuman strength, ability to fly, and magic powers. These magic powers come from lime, betel nut and stone axes. They have long hair which makes strange eerie sounds whistling in the wind. Brains are their favorite food.

The warrior women come from an island other than Malaita. Their skin is light. A large group, they all live together in a house similar to a men's house. They are smart, powerful, and fearless. Attracted by the large reward they join in the effort to win back the wives from the evil ghosts. Using their feminine wiles and powerful feminine essence, they make the evil ghosts powerless, and take back the abducted wives. They also use a weapon not commonly used in Malaita, a boomerang.

In this story they beat the drum, an activity forbidden for women, and get away with it. As a reward for success in battle, the leader of the women leaves the traditional prizes to her group of women and takes an unusual prize for herself.

This tale shows the duality of attitudes toward women, from wives to powerful warriors. To their credit the wives showed strength-in avoiding the sexual advances and the food offered by the ghosts, but the warrior women were powerful enough to vanquish the ghosts.

There is great ambivalence in the way Malaitan men view women as seen in the contrast between these warrior women and the women in the previous stories. Here is a recognition of women's power, yet a desire to keep it controlled. The warrior women are not from Malaita, so Malaitan women need not identify with them.

WARRIOR WOMEN AND GHOSTS

Two young married women, Raronaia and Araanaia, were walking through Aigarue when they caught the attention of two ghosts *gosile*, who were cruising through the clouds above. One ghost, Otabulau, said to the other, Nuitarara, "You jump down on the woman behind while I jump on the woman in front." They flew down, lifted the women onto their shoulders, and flew off with them to their home on top of a rock in the sea. Each ghost set his woman down near the area where food was prepared. The women were quiet until each ghost held up a sharp axe saying, "We want to cut you up." Hearing this the women screamed, "You must not eat us. You must take care of us." As they continued to cry, Otabulau stroked Araanaia's breast with his axe. The two women screamed so loudly that the ghosts felt sorry for them and decided to give them food instead of killing them.

Gosile eat uncooked human flesh, but for the women they caught fish, cooked them on the rocks below, and brought them up to the house on top of the rock. After they had eaten some fish Otabulau explained a plan. "We want to cut one arch of one foot of each of you so your blood will flow out, your bodies will become light, and you will be able to fly. Then no other gosile will be able to catch and eat you." The women agreed, so this was done to both of them. However, then the ghosts ordered each woman to stay inside the house.

While the women rested there, the gosile caught the women's brothers-in-law, killed them, and ate them, saving a small piece of each body which they brought to the two women. The women refused the food, saying, "This is forbidden to us. In our village we do not eat men. Today we are leaving!"

By this time the husbands of the two women, Gwaufiu and Uluirara, had put up blood money, hoping to capture whoever had stolen their wives. They, with their friends and relatives, gathered coconuts, betel nut seedlings, choice taro, pigs with tusks growing in circles, porpoise teeth, and one hundred strings of shell money as a reward for the return of their wives. Gwaufiu also gathered together one hundred canoes, and a large group of men went out to sea searching. The two ghosts spotted the large group of canoes, flew down, carried off two of the men and ate them.

The canoes returned to Anogwae, and the news of what had happened spread until Riina, leader of a group of light-skinned warrior women, heard about it. She decided to find out more information by going to Anogwae to question Gwaufiu. Arriving there she asked, "Is it true that the gosile caught the women near here?" She was told the story of how the women were taken by the gosile in nearby Aigarue. A group of girls in Anogwae cautioned her, "Though your arms and legs are strong, all your fighting strength is not equal to catching two gosile." This made Riina angry. She jumped up, stamped her foot, and vowed, "Although gosile, and male gosile at that, I shall break their jaws!"

Riina and her group of female relatives went hunting for the gosile. They inquired at several islands without success. Finally they reached Saraainonganogna, the home of the gosile. Nearing the shore, they heard the eerie sound of gosile hair crying in the wind. Riina's companions said, "Hide!" and Riina replied, "You hide. I will stand up in the canoe and wait for them." The gosile saw Riina and flew down to her, each carrying a stone axe. Otabulau took her head, Nuitarara her legs, and they swung their axes at her. But Riina freed her legs and grabbed Otabulau's hair by the roots then threw him into the canoe. Her companions brought out ten ropes braided from coconut husks and used these to tie his legs.

Then Riina asked him as he was lying in the canoe, "Please tell me, what is your power?" He replied, "My powers are from ginger, lime, and a stone axe." He stood up in the canoe and ginger came out of one ear, lime from another, and his red stone axe fell from his mouth. When these three items were on the bottom of the canoe, Riina stepped over them, contaminating them with her womanly presence, making them powerless. Having accomplished this, she turned on the charm, suggesting a friendship pact and asking him more about his powers. They began tying knots together.

They traveled by canoe back to where the gosile lived on a sharp rock in the sea. Arriving at the shore and seeing how high up the house was, Riina said, "My friend, your house is high and steep. How will I climb up? Why don't you fly to the top of the rock with this rope and tie it to the poison tree up there."

Otabulau did so, and she climbed up to his home on top of the rock. Going inside she saw rows of skulls covered with moss. There were eight rows of skulls with eight skulls in each row. The two of them walked among the rows of skulls until they came to one man's skull which was still bloody. "Are you still eating this head?" she inquired. "Yes," he replied.

Reaching the door of his shelter, Riina stepped in and sat down where Otabulau prepared his food. "Don't sit there," he cried, "That's a forbidden area." He didn't want a woman sitting on his eating area and defiling it. "I just arrived and don't know everything about your house, so don't be angry," answered Riina innocently.

When Araanaia and Raronaia saw Riina they cried for joy at finally being discovered. Riina asked them if they were married to the two gosile. "Definitely not," was their response. Suddenly Riina brought out a boomerang and slit Otabulau's head. The other ghost, Nuitarara, started to attack, but Riina also killed him. Looking around the house, she kicked down the rows of skulls until every one had fallen down. Then she carried down the bodies of the ghosts and put them into the canoe. The wives followed.

After paddling for six days the warrior women reached home where they shouted out the good news about the death of the ghosts and beat the drum with the triumphant warrior's drum call. Riina's sisters said, "Since you killed the ghosts and returned with the stolen wives we will all collect the prize money put up by Raronaia's and Araanaia's husbands."

The group of fighting women left their home, Kwaana Ae, also named Lumalao, and traveled with the two wives to their home at Anogwae. The husbands were waiting with the large reward which included one hundred pigs, porpoise teeth strung on the rafters, and bundles of vegetables and coconuts. Uluirara held out a bunch of betel nuts and welcomed Riina with a ritualized welcoming speech. She took the betel nuts from him with such force that she skinned his hand.

Riina then announced, "The prize which you are giving to me, give instead to my group of women. However, there is one thing that I would like. Give me the spirit of Taraboina." This was a house-abiding spirit belonging to Gwaufiu which was wise and could talk. So it was given to her, and the group of women gathered up their prizes and returned to their large home, Lumalao. Riina took the spirit of Taraboina and kept it in their house.

WARRIOR WOMEN — EXPLANATION
TOLD BY SEDEA AND BAURO, AUGUST 1967

Here is another tale of the powerful, light-skinned warrior women. Their home is described as being near a clearing surrounded by *ai ni gao* trees, a valuable ebony-type wood used for clubs which is native to Santa Isabel. This island to the northwest of Malaita may be the warrior women's home.

Rather than fighting evil spirits, this story is involved with feuding clans. The warrior women join some male relatives to kill men responsible for the deaths of their relatives. To overcome the enemy, one of the warrior women uses betel nuts with aphrodisiac powers plus her feminine wiles. Thus diverted, these men are vanquished by the warrior women's male relatives.

When the warrior women announce the victory by drum call, their male relatives are appalled by this breaking of a tabu-women are not allowed to beat the drum. The drum is a serious means of communication among the living and is also used to communicate with one's ancestors. The men decide not to give the warrior women the prize money as promised. Instead the men offer a pig to their ancestral ghosts to atone for this breaking of a tabu.

Ancestors listen carefully to drum messages. Certain patterns of drum beats inform the ancestral ghosts of memorial feasts to be held in their honor, so drums must not be tampered with by women.

But now the women are angry and with the help of a boomerang kill all of the men except one little boy who is staying in a decorated men's house. However, a large bird comes to the rescue. It turns over a tree root, red water then flows from the tree over the ancestral dance ground where the men's bodies lie. Crocodiles and snakes in the water bring the men back to life.

Tree roots again are conduits of magic power, as also found

in the stories *Balairi* and *Two Sisters Bulifoia and Fulifoia*. Since in this story the tree is in the sacred ancestral grove, it would have special powers from the ancestors.

Ancestral groves are visible for miles. Though the entire countryside is covered with bushes, vines and trees, these sacred stands of huge uncut timber are awe inspiring. Called *beu abu* (sacred men's house) the ancestors reside there.

Though the men are killed by women, since they are on good terms with their ancestral ghost, they are brought back to life. The ancestral ghost is more powerful than the warrior women.

Folktale motifs: Magic tree
Tabu of touching flowers
Resuscitation by magic

WARRIOR WOMEN

In a faraway place called Kwaana Ae, and also known by the names Manaili, Fiunarobo, Lumalau, and Manafia, many light-skinned women warriors lived in the style of house usually used only by men. One day the leader of this group, Moaanawalo, spoke to the women, saying "Take fishing nets and catch one hundred fish to take to market." They caught many more than one hundred fish and cooked some for dinner. Then they gathered together in a clearing surrounded by valuable hardwood trees *ai ni gao*. Their leader Moanawalo warned them, "Kwaria from Madumoa, may attack me at the market tomorrow and I may not return." Kwaria belonged to a group of cannibals who were noted for not being able to sleep if they had not eaten any human flesh.

The next morning Moaanawalo and three sisters went to the market by canoe and saw Kwaria and his group of warriors advance toward them with a dancing step. Kwaria asked

Moaanawalo how she got her special magic fighting powers. She did not answer directly, but pointed out he had killed a relative of hers, Onoiburi. He begged her not to be his enemy and asked for a betel nut from her handbag as a token of friendship. So Moaanawalo gave him a bunch of special betel nuts. Kwaria bit into one and gave some of the others to his friends. These betel nuts had aphrodisiac powers and Kwaria was suddenly filled with desire for Moaanawalo. After an afternoon of talking and flirting, they made plans to meet again in six days. Because Moaanawalo wanted a large group, it was agreed that she would bring 1080 women with her and Kwaria would bring a similar number of men. She coyly said she would see if her mother approved of her marrying him. At this idea, Kwaria was deliriously happy.

The girls returned home to prepare to meet Kwaria in six days. Riina, Moaanawalo's sister, went to talk to Gwauafu, the younger brother of Onoiburi who had been killed by Kwaria, to enlist his help in getting revenge. They came to an agreement that he and his men would help the warrior women fight Kwaria at the market.

In preparation for battle Moaanawalo retreated to her garden where magic plants grew. She broke off leaves of five magic plants. Then taking hold of a small special tree, she said to it, "If Kwaria is going to kill me you must shake. If he is not going to kill me, your head will break off." After she finished speaking, the top of the tree fell off, which she picked up and hung on her back and shared the magic leaves with all of her women. Then Riina tied a married woman's apron on Moaanawalo and bedecked her with shell ornaments.

When Kwaria arrived at the marketplace the girls were waiting and Kwaria was enchanted with the sight of Moaanawalo. Riina told him Moaanawalo would be his bride. The group of men and women socialized and chewed betel nut together on the sandy shore.

Meanwhile, Gwauafu, brother of the murdered Onoiburi, and his men surrounded the group on the beach. At noon, when the shadows were tiny, Gwauafu and his brothers screamed out a war cry. The girls attacked, Gwauafu's group attacked, and all of Kwaria's men were killed except Kwaria and three brothers. Moaanawalo planned to take them as captives back to her home, but on the way the four men were killed by a woman, Finirobo. But Moaanawalo went on home with the bodies.

Arriving home, Riina announced the victory by drum call, an activity forbidden to women. Gwauafu heard the women giving the drum call and was afraid and angry with Riina and Moaanawalo for beating the drum. He decided to sacrifice a pig to his ancestral spirit so the spirit would not be angry because the drum tabu had been broken. He also decided not to give the blood money of one hundred pigs, porpoise teeth, and shell money which he had previously agreed upon for the capture of Kwaria, the murderer of his brother. Instead, he stole the bodies of the four men from Moaanawalo's village, cut them up and cooked them along with the pigs he had promised to Moaanawalo.

When Moaanawalo heard that Gwauafu did not plan to give her the prize money she was furious, because to win the prize, she had dressed up as a married woman, tabu for an unmarried girl. She vowed to kill the next man from Gwauafu's village who came to her village, to atone for this wrong done to her.

While Gwauafu was eating the pigs that were to be his blood money to Moaanawalo, his ancestral spirit came and spoke to him, saying he should build a men's house and decorate it. The house was built, and Gwauafu appointed his younger brother, Kilaabu, to stay alone in the house as required by custom when a new men's house was completed. There Kilaabu would go through special ceremonies involving betel nut, leaves, and pigs.

Kilaabu stayed there alone for six days; no woman saw him. Then he noticed the faint scent of magic flowers. This fragrance was so captivating he decided to find and pick these flowers. Following the scent he traveled by a hidden path until he reached the warrior women's magic garden. Finding the fragrant tree he took out his fish lines and began stringing two strings of the flowers. As he shook the flowering tree which was named *kene fai nia* (woman with him), the wind carried the scent to Moaanawalo. She asked, "Who picked and crushed the magic flowers to make their fragrance drift through the forest?" She went to investigate and found Gwauafu's brother Kilaabu, stringing the flowers of the magic plant. She was so angry, she threw him on the ground, kicked in his ribs, and killed him. This was retribution for having put on the married woman's apron to assist Gwauafu in his battle with Kwaria and then not receive blood money.

Riina announced this death by drum. Gwauafu heard it and wondered what man the warrior women had killed this time. When he found out that it was his brother, he cried bitterly. His decorated men's house remained desolate and empty. Gwauafu thought about the feast he was to give in honor of his new house; he no longer cared to give it. Then his ancestral spirit spoke to him, saying he should have the feast even though his younger brother had been killed. So, Gwauafu sent his small son Tailangi, to live in the house to take the place of his dead brother Kilaabu.

Gwauafu dug up taro and gathered coconuts to prepare for the feast. He sent his wife to tell the warrior women to attend the feast. When his wife arrived at the home of the warrior women, they looked at her suspiciously, "Is the news good or bad?" they asked. She extended the invitation to the feast, and the warrior women laughed saying, "Gwauafu is lying; this is a trap."

Moaanawalo counted eighty of her 1,000 warriors who were willing to go with her. They traveled to Gwauafu's village and ate the feast food. They had decided not to begin any hostilities but to be on the lookout for a secret attack.

In the sacred grove of trees Moaanawalo secretly damaged some spears and also broke three roots of an *ai ni gao* tree. Later Moanawalo and Gwauafu argued about the wrongs done to each other, Moanawalo having put on the married woman's apron to help Gwauafu kill Kwaria and not receive the promised payment, and Gwauafu the murder of his brother.

A dance with panpipe music began. During the dance Moaanawalo threatened to spear Gwauafu in the throat if he did anything wrong. He said nothing, but he had told his dancers while dancing to surround the women and attack.

Gwauafu began the fight by throwing Moaanawalo on the ground. Their priest counseled the men to kill the women at once, or they would be killed themselves. Then Moaanawalo threw Gwauafu to the ground, took out a boomerang and hit him in the head. The women won, killing all the men. They piled up the dead bodies, then searched for the wife of Gwauafu. She begged for mercy, reminding them that she was originally from their village. But they told her, "Eat excrement," and murdered her, putting her body on top of her husband's.

Meanwhile, Gwauafu's young son Tailangi was still staying alone in the decorated men's house. When his father did not come to see him, he began to cry. A huge bird named Korognugnunu who lived on top of a rock in the sea where the sun rises saw Tailangi weeping. This bird flew around the dance ground looking at the battleground, then landed on the branch of a tree named *sateana* in front of the men's house where Tailangi was staying. When it asked Tailangi why he was crying the boy was afraid to answer. The bird gave him the bad news of the death of everyone in his village.

Then this bird flew to the sacred grove of trees, Gwauafu's ancestral grove. He turned over a tree root; red water flowed from it, and creatures that bite (sharks, centipedes, crocodiles) came out. The water flooded completely over the dance ground where the dead men lay. The crocodiles and snakes cured the men and made them living again. Then the bird returned to the tree root and sent away the biting creatures.

The men awoke, returned home, and the bird flew back to the top of the rock in the middle of the sea.

Two Sisters Bulifoia and Fulifoia — Explanation
Told by Sedea and Bauro, June 1967

The problems of these two sisters begin when they talk to boys instead of doing their work. In this extremely puritanical society such freedom is not tolerated. Then embroiled in a generational conflict with their mother, instead of being submissive or committing suicide, they run away. The older sister Bulifoia leads their rebellious escape into the forest. There they are subject to magic powers that reach them through tree roots. While under the influence of these powers they become killers until more magic restores their good sense. This idea of ghostly power being transmitted by tree roots, as in the previous story, points out the immense influence of the forest. The gigantic trees, the fierce tropical storms, the overwhelming, all-pervasive green forest, dwarf humans in scale and power. And the powers of both known and unknown wild spirits who lurk in the remote forest make it additionally dangerous.

When Bulifoia is eventually located by her family she refuses a large gift sent by her mother. This is a rare instance in these tales where people refuse prize money or a gift of shell valuables. Bulifoia's husband is willing to accept the gift, but Bulifoia insists on rejecting it. Since bride-price has never been paid for her, when she insists that her husband refuse her family's gift, in effect he is giving bride-price to her family. Perhaps this was Bulifoia's motive, or perhaps she wished to be alienated from her family forever, still not having forgiven her mother after many years.

Balairi appears briefly in this story as do cousins of Abarialasi, so all three stories must be from about the same era. Ideas not stated, but that emerge from this tale, are that disobedient girls are alienated from their families, and mothers who are too unkind may lose their daughters forever.

WOMEN

Folktale motifs: Use of magic
Quest for lost sister

Two Sisters Bulifoia and Fulifoia

Taeaasi and her husband Abunilonga lived in Gwanafilu with their two adolescent daughters, Bulifoia and Fulifoia. The parents were very strict and forbade the girls to even speak to any man in Walelangi territory. The two girls obeyed their parents for a long time. But one day their mother said, "My two children, I am going to the garden, stay here until midday, then come to the garden and take some taro home and cook it for supper." After their mother had left, the two girls took bamboo containers and went to gather water. On their way they found Balari at home, and she joined them. At the spring, they met three young men who asked them to move away from the splashing water until they had finished drinking.

Bulifoia moved away, but not too far. As one of the boys, Osiailu, was drinking water from the bamboo spout, he noticed her beautiful breasts and began to flirt with her. "We can't stay here and talk," Bulifoia said, "it's too public. Let's go far into the forest." "That's too far away," Osiailu replied, "Let's go around on the other side of this stone cliff." For the rest of the afternoon the six of them lingered there and the girls did not get home at the usual time.

Bulifoia and Fulifoia's parents returned home from the garden and found the house empty. No water had been brought, no taro was cooked. They sent a nephew Uura to bring back some water to make soup. Balari saw him, was frightened and ran out of sight. Uura noticed the girls, and calmly filled his bamboo containers, but then suddenly struck Fulifoia and Bulifoia with a large stick. "You are not our brother, what right have you to hit us?" This remark made Uura furious, and he kicked them both so they fell into the water. Bulifoia fell in an awkward position with her legs apart (Baegu girls should never be seen this way) and she was ashamed to be seen by the boys after this awkward fall. Uura went home and told the girls' mother what had happened. When Bulifoia and Fulifoia reached home their mother screamed, "You two were courting were you, with men from our clan? You two will go hide in the bush, will you, until you are pregnant from the sky (illegitimately pregnant)!" Bulifoia retorted, "You did the same thing when you were a girl!" The mother, furious at this response, picked up a digging stick and rammed her daughter in the head. Though blood spurted from Bulifoia's head, her mother screamed, "You lie! Get out, if you talk like that — leave!"

The two girls cried all night and were unable to eat. In the morning their mother told them, "I am going to the garden. Come there later in the day." Both parents left for their garden. When alone, Bulifoia said to her younger sister, "I'm leaving because mother hit me so hard. Let's both leave our mother and father and go away from this place." Bulifoia took out a long porpoise tooth necklace that belonged to their mother. They counted the teeth, then cut the necklace in half creating two necklaces with 5,000 teeth each. Wearing their necklaces, they left home and began walking around the forest in Marado. Though they both became homesick, they were afraid to return home. "We must hide from everyone because if anyone sees us, they will stop us," cautioned Bulifoia. Their long secret journey took them into the most remote areas of the forest. Once they nearly ran into Abarialasi's cousins Manumarakwa and Oliolikona, but quickly hid from them. They crossed the little Kwara'ae River. When they arrived at the mouth of the large Kwara'ae River, the tide was in and they could not wade across. They decided to swim. In order to keep their belongings dry which they were carrying in woven baskets, as they swam they held their baskets up over their heads with sticks.

Reaching the other side of the river, Bulifoia looked back at the mountain ridge of northern Malaita and thought, I am leaving my homeland forever. Then turning to her sister, she told her to go on ahead. Picking up a stick she obliterated their footprints in the sand. Speaking to their ancestral ghosts, she said, "If our brothers are following us here from Marado, make them return and follow us no longer." Their secret journey had lasted for four months.

They continued on until they saw a frail man named Faibulua with an axe over his shoulder approaching them. They were not afraid and did not hide. "Where are you two good-looking girls from?" he inquired. Bulifoia told him to go on, but as he passed by she grabbed his axe, saying she wanted to use it to make her own axe. Seeing how strong the two girls looked, he did not argue. After cutting two axe handles, Bulifoia returned the axe and sent him on his way down the path.

At a riverbank, looking for some sharp stones, they found two suitable for axe heads. Bulifoia spoke to her ancestral ghost asking for power to break the stones into an axe shape. The spirit gave them the power, the stones were broken into axe shapes, and they tied them onto their axe handles. With their new axes they spent the night by a large tree named *faimela*. While they were sleeping, rain fell in the middle of the night. They heard thunder, but did not seem to be getting wet so they went back to sleep. A living ghost *akalo mauri* from their home in Gwaunafilu flew down to the treetop and put a special power in the tree. The rain carried this power down through the tree to the ground and into the mats on which the girls slept. Some of this water with its evil power entered their chests. When they awoke, they were insane. In the morning they picked up their axes and traveled on until they met an old man. They killed him. Later in the middle of the Kwara'ae forest near Fufula (boiling water) they killed a man named Urikene (live with woman). That night the living ghost returned and told Bulifoia he was restoring her and her sister's good sense so they would be able to think clearly again.

The next morning the girls went down to the seashore. Since it was low tide, they made baskets from coconut fronds and went out on the reef to gather conch shells. They gathered shells until their baskets were filled.

A man named Daoboroboro from Ano Ano who had also gone out on the reef that morning saw them collecting shells. Wondering where these two beautiful girls had come from, he hid behind a rock to watch them more closely.

The girls noticed him spying on them and approached. He asked, "Where do you come from?" Bulifoia put down her basket of conch shells, picked up her axe and struck Daoboroboro. He was startled, as though seeing a ghost. His neck was broken, his head flopped backwards, but he did not die because he knew black magic. Now the girls trembled with fright. Daoboroboro spoke some words to his spirit of black magic and his head sat upright again. Then he threatened them, "If you attack me, it is you who will die of a broken neck." They were frightened into submission.

Finding Bulifoia attractive, he led the girls to his home in Ano Ano. When they had nearly arrived he told the sisters to wait in the forest. He went on ahead and explained to his two brothers what had happened. He sent them out to look at the girls, saying Bulifoia was going to be his, but perhaps one of them might be interested in her younger sister.

Bulifoia became Daoboroboro's wife and Fulifoia married one of his younger brothers. Houses were built and they settled into married life. However, Fulifoia later became ill and died.

Meanwhile, back in Gwaunafilu, the girls' parents Abuilonga and Taeaasi offered a large reward for any information about their daughters. A group of men searched far and wide across Malaita but found no trace of them.

Daoboroboro asked his friend Turubui from Langalanga territory to travel to Lau territory to buy roasted almonds for making feast food to celebrate the new house he had just finished building for his wife.

Traveling in a white canoe and carrying shell money to buy food, Turubui went north stopping at various markets along the coast. In Bita'ama he collected 3,000 canarium almonds. At the market in Ae na Bubulo he bought a huge pig from Kwawalafa, a brother of the two girls. While Kwawalafa was collecting the shell money for the pig, he said to Turubui, "You are a man from Langalanga territory which faces Kwaio territory, has there been any news of two girls coming there? I am searching for my two sisters." Turubui answered that his friend Daoboroboro had recently married a beautiful woman whose sister had died, and no one knew where these sisters were from. In fact, the food he was buying was for a feast to celebrate Daoboroboro's new house. Kwawalafa asked if he could return with Turubui and meet Daoboroboro's bride.

Turubui and Kwawalafa traveled in the white canoe to Langalanga territory. Meanwhile Daoboroboro and Bulifoia went down to the market on the coast to wait for Turibui to return.

When Bulifoia looked up and saw her brother in the canoe she cried, "What ghost brings you here that I see you again?" She took her brother to her new home. A large feast of pigs and taro and almond pudding was prepared for the housewarming party. Kwawalafa stayed for a four-month visit before returning home. As he left he invited Bulifoia to go back with him for a visit, but Bulifoia had a baby by this time and was not willing to make the trip.

Kwawalafa returned home and told his parents about Bulifoia's life, her husband and child. Their mother Taeaasi called on all her relatives in Marado to collect shell money to give to

Daoboroboro for caring for her long lost daughter whom she had given up for dead. When the valuables were collected, Kwawalafa, Taeasalo, the older sister of Taeaasi, and eighty men carried the shell valuables to Daoboroboro.

When they arrived with the gift, Daoboroboro accepted it, but Bulifoia refused it, saying, "I left my mother, I am angry with her, you must take back this money. There is no friendship between us. We are too far apart."

Kwawalafa went back home again carrying the gift money that Bulifoia had refused. The mother and father were stunned at the return of the gift. Taeaasi said, "I am too old to travel, I will not see her again since she is so far away, but you, Kwawalafa, must talk to her again."

HEROES

LAENIMOTA AND ABARIALASI — EXPLANATION
TOLD BY SEDEA AND BAURO, JUNE 1967

Laenimota is a handsome, somewhat lazy man; a culture hero who uses a love potion to win his beautiful wife. Later when she is abducted by a Polynesian man, he perseveres until he finds and kills the Polynesian and wins her back. He also becomes entangled with a woman Oorobila (too dirty) who forces him to perform oral intercourse. He manages to have her killed.

Laenimota is the strongest character is this tale. His wife Abarialasi is a woman whose life is ruled by the men around her. The amphibian turtle is important since it carries Laenimota between several worlds, the Melanesian and the Polynesian, land and sea, and air and water. The turtle also sets limits as to where eating can take place, perhaps a reference to a tabu on oral intercourse.

Birds are also important. One arranges Laenimota's ride with the turtle, another outwits Oorobila.

High in the hills above our village, hidden on an overgrown sidepath, is a rock called Abarialasi. On the flat side of this large rock a nearly life-size stick figure of a woman has been carved. Her legs are spread so far apart that the soles of her feet are touching and her arms point to her genitals where a hole has been carved.

The posture of this woman's image is a rebellion against the strict rules women follow of sitting gracefully while wearing a pubic apron. Traditionally pagan women must sit and stand carefully in order to be properly modest. While showing me this image Lebefiu explained that each leg of the woman's figure was referred to as sasafa which means thigh. Since the Sasafa River runs down the center of the eastern half of Baegu territory, perhaps the banks of the river are thought of as thighs and the whole eastern Baegu territory is viewed as a huge woman, a mother earth.

Folktale motifs: Love potions
Love at first sight
Helpful birds
Turtle carrying man on back
Rocks open and close

LAENIMOTA AND ABARIALASI

Laenimota was a young man who had been ordered by his elders to plant a taro garden and to watch over it carefully until the taro ripened. He was forbidden during this time to take a bath, go to market, cut his hair, be seen by a woman, or go anywhere except between the men's house and his garden. The taro would not ripen for three months.

For many days he did as he was told, thinking only of his garden, how he was forced to work to grow food to feed many men. He thought, "I don't like being tabu with this garden. One month of this is enough." So he picked up a red flint stone, walked out of the men's house, and went downhill to the house of his sister Daroabu. He walked in saying, "Daroabu, please cut my hair." She asked, "Why do you come here? I must not even see you because you're tabu with your taro garden. You will make me die because of this!"

"You all can take care of that garden. I'm tired of it." Then he threatened her, "I'll do something terrible if you refuse to cut my hair." Daroabu was frightened, but replied, "I don't care to cut your hair." "Then I'll step over your legs (a ritual defilement) if you won't!" Daroabu, hearing this, picked up the sharp stone, gazed steadily out to sea, and cut his hair. Then she put some bark onto the glowing embers in the fireplace. When the fire flared up, she put the clippings of Laenimota's hair into the fire. Then she washed her hands to remove all traces of the haircut and said, "Stand over there in the light so I can see how you look." Admiring his appearance, she kidded him, "If you were not my brother, I'd flirt with you!"

Laenimota returned to the men's house in upper Mota, picked up some rope, and fashioned a belt for himself. When finished, he set out a long wooden bowl and poured some water into it from a bamboo container. He looked at himself in this water mirror, then took eight white cowrie shells, strung them onto a string, and wove them into his hair. He put on a necklace of large porpoise teeth, picked up his war club *alofolo*, and went out. He stopped in the doorway of the girls' house, and Daroabu asked, "Where are you going?" He replied, "To Siubogi (a hamlet on the other side of the island)."

In the late afternoon he arrived at the watering place of that hamlet where he met a group of girls, cousins of his, gathering water in bamboo tubes. He asked, "Why are you collecting all this water?" Alabuma, the daughter of his father's sister, inquired, "You are tabu with your taro garden. When will the first fruits ceremony take place?" He replied, "I didn't ask you to ask about that garden. All this water you're getting, what is it for?" She replied, "We are bringing water to 'Ore'Ore and Aebusu where we will wait for canoes." When Laenimota heard this, he laughed for joy, "Are you going to a feast?" She answered, "Not to a feast. We are going to the *faa baita* ceremony for Abarialasi."

They all got into canoes. Memenia, a brother of the girls, said, "You should go back home to Mota and stay with your taro garden, not go on with us to Talufie (Abarialasi's home)." Laenimota paid no attention to this advice. The group paddled to the river mouth at Malifoa, then went by foot to Abarialasi's home, arriving in the early evening.

A crowd of men and women had already gathered. One young man said, "We should all stand around the house so Abarialasi can see us." Another said, "Today we are gathering to sing to Abarialasi, let us begin." The young men went into her house and sat down in two lines facing each other. While they were singing they each kept time by precisely clicking together two small bamboo sticks. They had also decorated their hair with shells to make the best possible impression. Abarialasi sat on her bench and watched them for two hours but did not see one man who appealed to her. She didn't care for any man there.

During this time Laenimota was busy making a love potion, known in his home in Mota, from the bud of the wanealisa plant. He told Alabuma to bring him some water. After she brought him the water, he went into the forest alone and mixed water with this special plant. He washed his body with this potion, then returned to his cousins saying, "Let's go watch the singing; it's nearly daybreak."

Arriving there, he stood behind a group of his cousins, including Manumarakwa and Oliolikona, watching the chanting. By this time the two rows of men were swaying in unison, caught in a hypnotic trance. When Abarialasi looked up and suddenly saw Laenimota, she immediately knew he was the one her heart desired. Then he disappeared. She cried for him, but did not speak. Her heart was shut tightly; she would have no one but him. Finally when the chanting was over, she spoke. "I have seen many men, all the young men who have come here, but the man I saw standing behind Manumarakwa is the one who will be my husband. I will have only him. Send for him to come to me so we can eat betel nut together."

But Laenimota had run away because he was shy and afraid of what he had done with the love potion. But Manumarakwa found him and told him, "Even though you are nervous, you must go see her. But Laenimota replied, "I don't have any money. How can I marry her without bride-price?" "Even though you have no money, you must go to her, since she loves you," Manumarakwa insisted. Then an older relative offered, "Since you have no money, we will buy this woman for you since she loves you and you are part of our clan." They gave Laenimota twenty strings of shell money and many porpoise teeth necklaces so he could buy his bride.

Laenimota bought his bride, and the two of them traveled back toward Mota. When they arrived at the edge of the clearing around his home, he told her, "Stay here. If any woman comes by, let her come to you." He went on to his sister's house. Daroabu said, "You who just came back from the other side of the island, give me some betel nut please." Laenimota replied, "Go bring the bunch of betel nut I left on the edge of the path." Going for the betel nut, she discovered Abarialasi instead and gave a shout, "Laenimota, you've been kidding me. There's no betel nut here, there's a bride!" His other sister Sangaabu heard the news and took a bundle of mats and spread them out on the path from the house to where Abarialasi stood. Then Daroabu took Abarialasi's hand and formally led her over the mats to the doorway of the house.

Laenimota's mother was concerned that this bride might not have been properly paid for, so Laenimota explained how he had managed to buy Abarialasi. Then his mother brought out a shining shell disc married woman's belt and tied it around the bride's waist and Abarialasi also put on the blue married woman's apron. His mother also told him, "Even though you left your taro garden because you wanted a woman, we have kept your garden for you. We are not angry, you will live here with her in Mota." They lived together happily until several months later when the taro was ripe. At that time Laenimota's father Tofunigwauabu said to his son, "I want you to go to the market at Sulione and bring back some fish to eat with the taro from your garden."

CHAPTER II

Laenimota said to this wife, "You go to the market." So Abarialasi went with her sister-in-law Sangaabu to the market at Sulione. A Polynesian man named Alelemae from Sikiana Island held up a fish for Abarialasi to buy. As she reached for the fish, he grabbed her around the waist, held her tightly, and put her into his canoe even though she was a married woman. He quickly fled with her in his canoe.

Sangaabu returned home and told Laenimota what had happened. He was furious. No one knew this stranger who had abducted Abarialasi. Laenimota became despondent. He searched and searched for his wife on the seashore. Then he went up into the hills where he could overlook the sea where she had disappeared. He took a sharp stone and carved Abarialasi's image on a large stone that remains to this day.

After finishing the carving, he returned to the sea to search further for his wife. He found a turtle named *Fau Ni Gelegele* lying by a stream where it flowed into the sea. A bird *sisifiu* flew overhead and asked Laenimota, "What are you looking for?" "My wife," he answered. The bird told him, "You haven't seen her because she was stolen by Alelemae who has taken her to his home far away. Do you want to see her?" When Laenimota answered, "Yes," the bird asked for a present. Laenimota offered him shell money, pigs, and porpoise teeth, but the bird refused, saying he was not a man and did not care for that sort of thing. However, he would be pleased if he had some leaves of taro.

While Laenimota was returning home to get the taro leaves, a heavy rain began to fall. Seeking shelter, he stood by a large overhanging rock which happened to be the home of an evil woman, named Oorobila (literally — very dirty). Seeing Laenimota, she sharply struck the rock, and Laenimota was astonished to find himself enclosed in the rock. Oorobila laughed. "Who says you are a good man?" she taunted. "This is where I live." She came close to him and put her ass by his nose. "You lick my ass there. You must give me what I want to get out of this rock. Many licks you must give me." After he did what she requested, she again struck the rock. It opened, and he went outside. He angrily tried to strike Oorubila with his club *subi*, but it broke when it hit the rock. She had quickly made the rock close again and remained inside. He heard her mocking laughter echoing inside the rock.

He continued home to Mota and told his older brothers what had happened. In the morning he collected taro leaves and went with his sisters, who carried the taro leaves, back to the seashore. The turtle and the bird were waiting for Laenimota to return. The sisters put the bundles of taro on the sand. The turtle, instead of the bird, ate all of the leaves, then said he was ready to carry Laenimota to his wife. Laenimota told his sisters to go home, as he climbed up on the back of Fau Ni Gelegele. The turtle advised him, "If you get hungry, look for a floating coconut." Then the turtle cautioned him, "You may only eat over the bone by my neck. My tailbone is forbidden."

They went out to sea. Laenimota saw a coconut floating

toward him. He picked it up, and forgetting what Fau Ni Gelegele had told him, ate it over the tailbone. The turtle, angry at being disobeyed, dived deeply into the sea until he reached the sand at the bottom of the ocean. The bird *sisifiu*, which was accompanying them overhead, could not follow. Laenimota's breath was gone. He was nearly drowned when Fau Ni Gelegele surfaced with Laenimota still hanging onto his back. The turtle told him, "I frightened you because you disobeyed me." Laenimota's breath returned, and they continued on to the island of Matasilalo (Sikiana) and stopped at Sasafaugali, where Laenimota went ashore. Now the bird told him, "You must stay here. Search for your wife. Wait here for six days, at the end of six days I will return. If you see your wife, you may talk to her."

At dusk that day Alelemae said to Abarialasi, "Take this basket down to the beach and bring back some of the rocks there to make an oven to cook some fish." She went down by the passage in the reef and saw Laenimota. She cried with joy and asked, "How did you get to this place? But now I am living with Alelemae. I am married to him." He replied, "Even though you are, I am going to take you back with me."

Fau Ni Gelegele who was resting on the beach counseled Laenimota, "Kill everyone here." Laenimota took this advice and killed everyone on the island, including Alelemae. Then he made his wife his alone once again.

The turtle told them to get ready to go. Laenimota and Abarialasi climbed up on the back of Fau Ni Gelegele. Abarialasi sat by the turtle's tail while Laenimota sat by the neck. "Hold on tight. We are going to Malaita," announced the turtle. They returned home safely to Sulione then walked to Mota. Arriving home they described their adventures and Laenimota announced to everyone that though his wife had been abducted, she was again his wife and his alone.

Heroes

They lived happily together in Mota. But Laenimota was bothered by the awful memory of his experience with Oorobila. He decided to organize a fighting party to kill her. This group of men surrounded the rock where she lived, but she struck the rock and closed herself safely inside. Then laughing, she said, "You will kill me, will you?" The men were unable to enter the rock and returned home. However, Laenimota continued to search for some way of killing Oorobila, the woman who mocked him. He heard about a magical bird *tutuiau* with great power in Subea. He went there and spoke to Gwaegwae, the owner of the bird, who agreed to sell its power to Laenimota.

Gwaegwae got together a group of one hundred men, and carrying the magic bird, they surrounded Oorobila's rock. However, she was not inside since she had gone out searching for almonds. They left the bird on the ground in front of the rock. It scattered a pile of nuts she had left by her door. Rain began to fall and Oorobila, returning home, saw that the bird had scattered her nuts and was furious. Throwing the bundle that she was carrying to the ground, she picked up a walking stick and chased after the bird which began to cry "Tooooo Tooooo." The raiding party heard this and knew she was chasing after the bird, which kept just out of reach, leading her far away from her rock. In the meantime, the men went inside her rock. When she returned, they picked up clubs, hit her and cracked her skull until she died.

The raiding party went to Mota and told everyone about the death of Oorobila. They beat the drum and spread the news with the drum call Tatae Abu, (many fast drum beats followed by a warwhoop). Laenimota gave them one hundred strings of shell money since he was very pleased.

SOLOMON ISLAND FOLKTALES FROM MALAITA

NIDURAMO — EXPLANATION

TOLD BY SEDEA, LEBEFIU AND BAURO, SEPTEMBER 1967

This popular folktale was a favorite at all-night singing sessions. The main character, the culture hero Niduramo, is a warrior who performs remarkable feats of strength and skill. He also liberally uses magic to achieve his goals. A love potent helps him win his bride, Raonioa, though her relatives had already promised her to someone else. Magic plants then make people sleepy and allow the couple to flee.

Raonioa, in the first half of the story, is also a strong personality. She kills the husband chosen for her by her relatives and goes off with her true love. Later when the pair run into the evil ghost Ulu Ulu Matakwa, she ties his long hair to a coconut tree so Niduramo can kill him.

Then the couple go to another island, the home of Wane Dududu, to collect the prize money this important man had offered for the death of the evil ghost. The people here are light-skinned, have different dances, different evil spirits, and different burial traditions.

Niduramo brings home prize-laden canoes and two light-skinned wives. He should live happily ever after. But all of his skills as a warrior and ability to gather prize money do not carry him on to greater fame and fortune. Instead he makes the worst possible mistake. He forgets to honor his ancestors with a memorial feast, and in their anger they let him die.

Folktale motifs: Magic formulae
Trying hair to prevent pursuit
Loss of fortune (death) for breaking rule

NIDURAMO

CHAPTER I

Buafera and other important, older men of the village of Abuoli forbade the young and beautiful girl Raonioa to touch, speak with, or flirt with any man. A large house was built for her and her older sisters with a special bed for Raonioa up in the rafters decorated with shell and porpoise teeth valuables. Buafera and his younger brothers kept watch around the house at night, looking for any man who might come to talk to Raonioa. For four months the house was guarded while the news spread of the beautiful girl who slept in a bed high in the rafters. Raonioa was the first woman in Malaita to sleep off the ground and everyone was talking about this woman.

In another part of the Malaita, a handsome young man, Niduramo, tiring of hearing about this girl without knowing what she looked like, decided to travel to her village. After walking for several days, he arrived at her house at mid-morning. Since everyone there had left to work in the gardens, the house was empty. He noticed all the footprints on the path near the top of Borofunga Mountain and decided to hide and wait there for the girl and her family to return late in the afternoon. Hearing them coming, he hid behind some trees and looked carefully at all the girls as they walked past in single file on the narrow path. He thought none of them was so very beautiful, then suddenly he saw her. He knew it must be Raonioa, the girl wearing a lavish porpoise teeth necklace. He was struck by the beauty of her face and figure and felt he was not nearly handsome enough for her.

Unnoticed he followed at a distance and saw Buafera close the gate of the fence around the village. Darkness fell and he continued to wait until everyone was quietly sleeping. But inside the house Raoniota, Raonioa's oldest sister, was still awake chewing betel nut. Niduramo stood outside the door and stamped his foot. She know it was a suitor when she peeked outside and saw Niduramo standing there wearing shell ornaments, his body shining like a ripe betel nut. She woke up her younger sisters except for Raonioa then asked him, "Where are you from that you dare to come here? Haven't you heard that Buafera has sworn that no man come stealthily to this house?" Niduramo answered that his name was Tafelo. Raoniota knew he was lying since that was her brother's name and said, "Tell me your real name or I will scream so Buafera will come and kill you!"

This made Niduramo angry. He kicked one of the posts supporting the roof. Dust and debris fell off the underside of the roof onto Raonioa who was still sleeping. She woke up. Hearing her sisters talking to Niduramo, she jumped down to the ground from her bed in the rafters, took up a torch, and went outside to see what was going one. Looking at Niduramo in the flickering light, she thought he was the most handsome man she had ever seen. The sisters asked him inside. He explained that he was from the other side of the island and that he had come to see the girl dedicated to virginity. In the darkness her older sister Raoniota held the torch up over Raonioa's head, "Here she is." Niduramo had bathed with a love potion, and suddenly Raonioa's heart was pierced at the sight of him.

She asked him to stay with her, and they made love during the middle of the night in the bed high in the rafters. Raoniota heard them and in the very early morning told Niduramo that he now must ask Raonioa to his home. "You have to marry her," she insisted.

Niduramo went outside and Raonioa followed. He gave her a porpoise teeth necklace he had been wearing and told her he would come back for her in ten days. He left as dawn was approaching and returned home to Buibasi. There he announced to his family he had seen the girl who was going to be his wife.

Meanwhile, Uikete and Irukete decided they needed to find a bride for their younger brother Dufa. Uikete visited Buafera, and the two important men sat in front of Buafera's men's house trading stories and chewing betel nut. Raonioa happened to walk past them while carrying water back from the spring, and Uikete noticing her immediately asked how much bride-price was required to buy her. "One hundred strings of red shell money and ten thousand porpoise teeth," replied Buafera. Despite this inflated bride-price, Uikete still wanted Raonioa for his younger brother. Buafera agreed that if Uikete brought him ten pigs and ten strings of red shell money she would be kept a virgin (literally the bow would be kept sacred) until he brought the remainder of the money.

A few days later Uikete and his relatives brought this initial payment while shouting and singing. "Who are they coming for?" asked Raonioa who had heard nothing about her arranged marriage. She trembled when she found out they were coming for her. When Buafera told her she was being given as a bride to Dufa, the tears flowed from her eyes. "You must give one of my sisters away instead!" she insisted. Then seeing it was hopeless to argue, she said no more. She returned to her house and in front of everyone there she spread one leg in one direction saying, "The women from my village can put the *obi* (red woven bracelet or anklet-a symbol of marriage) on this leg." Then she spread her other leg in the opposite direction (a very indecent, unladylike gesture since Malaitan women always stand and sit very modestly) saying, "The groom's family can put the obi on this leg." After this was done, they stayed around her and sang songs.

While this was going on, Niduramo was just returning to Raonioa's village. As he arrived at her house he wondered what was the cause of all the singing and feasting. When he found out that Raonioa was being sold, he was furious. Her older sister suggested that he might marry her instead, but he wasn't at all interested in Raoniota. Inside the crowded house Raonioa said she needed cooler air, excused herself and went outside where Niduramo at last found her alone. Angry, he asked for his necklace back since she was marrying someone else. She refused to return it, saying she hadn't made love to Dufa yet. "Let's run away," she begged.

Niduramo gave Raonioa a magic branch to put over the fire when she went back inside the house. The smoke from the fire caused everyone there to fall asleep. Then Niduramo gave Raonioa a *subi* club and together they killed many of the sleeping people. Next they stole the money Uikete was going to use for bride-price, and finally Raonioa woke up her husband-to-be, Dufa, and killed him with a blow of her club.

Niduramo beat the village drum, sending news of what had happened back to Niduramo's house. Leaving Raonioa's village Niduramo took his bride home to show her to his mother. She thought she was beautiful, but Niduramo's brothers knew there was trouble ahead, it would only be a matter of time before Buafera would come to fight with them.

Later when they heard that Buafera and his raiding party were on the way, Niduramo's mother put a plant in the path leading to their house which had the property of cooling emotions. Buafera stepped over the plant, was no longer angry, and returned home. Then he sent a message to Niduramo that a gift of money and pigs would be accepted. Niduramo agreed to send the gift and Buafera agreed that Niduramo would legally buy his bride.

However, some of Buafera's relatives, Aramae and Ilisau, were not satisfied with this arrangement. They continued to want to fight Niduramo.

In preparation for the marriage feast, Buafera gathered coconuts, betel nuts, taro, fish, crayfish, opossum, pigs, and birds. He asked his younger brothers to go and tell Niduramo and his bride to come to the feast and have the married woman's apron officially tied on by Raonioa's mother. But Niduramo being suspicious of Buafera refused to go, instead he sent his wife accompanied by his older brother, Abanafilu. They went back to Raonioa's home, and her mother officially tied on the married woman's apron. Abanafilu gave Raonioa's mother a present of long strings of shell money.

Meanwhile Aramae, who had gathered together eighty men, went up to Raonioa and said, "They made you a wife today (by tying on the married woman's apron), but I am taking you back with me. In my opinion, you are not legally Niduramo's wife." Raonioa tried to escape while Abanafilu and his men attacked Aramae's fighting party, but Aramae succeeded in carrying off Raonioa.

When the news reached Niduramo that Aramae had abducted Raonioa, Niduramo ran to Aramae's village and found her standing in a doorway. He took her back, killed forty men, and then returned home with his wife.

But now Buafera, the former peacemaker, said angrily, "My brother-in-law is a true warrior. He has killed many men in many places, but now he has killed some of my relatives." He told his people, "Everyone from today on must fight Niduramo even though he is my brother-in-law. He went with his men to attack Niduramo and his relatives. They fought, then Buafera withdrew with some losses and declared a time of truce.

During this quiet time Niduramo built a large house, and lived peacefully with Raonioa. Together they grew a large garden. Raonioa and Niduramo worked extremely hard and were able to feed many pigs.

CHAPTER II

One day instead of gardening they walked down to the shore and out into the shallow reef waters. Niduramo carried his bow and arrow while Raonioa carried her backpack. In the distance they noticed gulls feeding at a river mouth. Approaching the area, they saw large fish *longa* chasing small fish *buma* which were jumping up onto the sand. They caught many of these small fish which they later tied up in four hundred bundles. Niduramo built a log raft since he wanted to take the fish home by sea. Raonioa preferred to carry the fish and go by land but Niduramo told her to be quiet.

They anchored the raft by tying it to coconut palms while loading the fish, but a violent thunderstorm sent floodwaters rushing down from the mountains and uprooted the palms. The raft carrying Niduramo, Raonioa, and the bundles of fish drifted out to sea, eventually reaching the island Mutanasi, the home of evil ghosts *gosile*. Niduramo scouted around the island. No one appeared to be at home, but when they found a house full of bones they were afraid. Their arrival had been observed by the ghost Ulu Ulu Matakwa from the top of his rock home. He took up his axe, flew into the sky, and spoke to the thunder and clouds telling them to descend over Niduramo and Raonioa so they would not be able to see him approach. He came down by a coconut palm near where they were resting in a shelter they had built. Raonioa saw him first and woke up her husband. The gosile tore down their shelter. Niduramo fought fiercely with him. Raonioa noticed the gosile's long hair flying in the wind near the coconut trees. She tightly tied his hair to the trees. The gosile was strong, bared his teeth and shook his head, but could not loosen his hair. Niduramo struck him on the head and killed him. They admired and counted his enormous teeth, then lit a fire.

The smoke drifted over to Salokwalié, the home of Wane

HEROES

Dududu and his sons. Since gosile ate raw meat and did not cook, the fire was unusual, and the sons were sent to investigate. Arriving at the island they found Raonioa and Niduramo cooking a large bundle wrapped up in leaves. When the sons finally managed to find out what was wrapped in the bundle, they said, "Don't cook this gosile anymore. There is a big reward for his capture. Our father will give you one hundred pigs, ten thousand porpoise teeth, and two women as brides." Raonioa whispered to her husband, "This is a trick." "Be quiet," Niduramo replied.

By canoe they all took the gosile's body to the island where Wane Dududu lived. Unlike Malaita, people on this island had light skins. Wane Dududu was pleased at the death of the gosile Ulu Ulu Matakwa and as promised he gave the large reward to Niduramo, including two sisters named Mongaaia and Mongaalasa as brides. Niduramo asked Raonioa if she could agree to living with the two women if he accepted the girls. Raonioa replied that she wouldn't object, so Niduramo and his three wives spent six months together at Wane Dududu's village in a house provided for them. The three women slept on one side of the house, Niduramo on the other. After a while, one of the new wives complained to Raonioa, "Why doesn't he sleep with us? Tell him he should come to us this evening." That evening he talked with his two new wives and told them that he wasn't interested in sex. He only wanted to go home, then he could arrange for people there to bring their canoes to help him carry his large reward home with him to Buibasi.

Next morning Niduramo and his three wives made a secret trip by canoe to Niduramo's home. As they began their journey, one of his new brides, Mongaalasa, threw a coconut behind the canoe saying to the snake of the sea (*baekwa* or shark), "If you are powerful, lead this canoe to our destination." They arrived safely and Niduramo went ahead to speak with his relatives to ask for help in bringing home the prize pigs and valuables. But he spoke in a circuitous fashion saying, "Who among you is equal to building the house for which I just laid out the foundation?" When they eventually understood what he meant and how large the prize money was, twenty men took canoes at daybreak to help pick up the reward from Wane Dududu. Mongaalasa, again the last in the last canoe, threw out a coconut and spoke again in the same manner to the shark, asking for a safe journey. When their canoes landed on the beach, Wane Dududu was angry with the two girls for not telling him where they had gone on their secret journey. He told them he should have been informed so a welcoming group could have been there to greet the canoes. Many people were sent for and a large group gathered.

Preparations were made for Niduramo to dance a special dance with his bow, spear, and shield. The 100 prize pigs, strings of shell money, and 10,000 porpoise teeth were placed on the dance ground. The three wives stood facing the pigs. Then Niduramo and his three wives executed a complicated dance *kwangi*, which included the chanting of ritual speeches.

Anxious to get away, Niduramo had told his 20 men to load the canoes with the prize pigs and valuables while the dance was in progress. But one of the men watching the dance, Darogwau, suggested that since Niduramo had performed the kwangi dance, Wane Dududu should show Niduramo an evil spirit *akalo ta'a* before he departed. Though eager to leave, Niduramo had to wait while Wane Dududu went to his ancestor's sacred grove of trees and spoke to the spirit there saying, "If you are powerful, you must show yourself today so this crowd can see you." No sooner had he finished speaking when a rainbow bent around them. There were many short rainbows. One was red and made their bodies burning hot. Then another made their bodies cool and yellow. The people saw the beautiful colors and trembled with fear. Then Wane Dududu picked up a magic branch and made the rainbows disappear.

Canoes loaded, good-byes said, Wane Dududu counseled the two new wives to stay with their warrior husband and to obey him. So Niduramo returned home with Raonioa, prize-laden canoes, and two lovely new wives.

But peace and prosperity did not follow Niduramo's return. Buafera was jealous of Niduramo's success and gathered up a war party against him. Niduramo killed everyone in the group except Buafera.

The smell of all this blood made Mongaalasa ill. Such bloodshed was forbidden on Wane Dududu's island. Niduramo went to her sickbed. She got up, knelt before him, and bid him goodbye. She fell down, he felt her chest, but her breath was gone.

Niduramo discussed burial customs with her sister, Mongaaia. Niduramo's people buried their dead. Mongaaia's people put bodies on a bench over the sea. The rotting liquid from a body ran down into the sea and turned into a shark. So Mongaalasa was wrapped up and put on a bench over the sea.

Aramae (the man who once abducted Raonioa) came by, peeked into the bundle, and told his younger brother Dumuafea to carry it home to be cooked for food. As Dumuafea was carrying the body, it began to swell, and liquid leaked onto him. Because of this he caught the disease *luma asi* (literally — woman's house by the sea). His body became swollen, he couldn't walk. Then Niduramo killed him for stealing the body. Two other men tried to carry away Mongaalasa's body, but met the same fate. Mongaaia then fearlessly rescued the body of her sister and replaced it on the bench over the sea.

The fighting over, everyone rested and another peaceful period began. But during all of these successes as a warrior, Niduramo had forgotten what was most important. He had failed to give a feast in honor of his ancestors. His ancestors became more and more angry as they waited and waited. They decided to protect him no longer.

Niduramo became ill. He was taken to the women's house so his two wives could take care of him. His condition worsened, and Raonioa wept, knowing she would be left behind. In the middle of the night he asked for his son, named Buafera, to be brought to him. He touched the body of his small child, saying, "Buafera, you must say goodbye. I am about to die and will leave you. The ancestral spirits of Buibasi and Anoanonoro are letting me go. I have fought many battles because of your mother." He told his two wives to look after his son and feed him well. Then his breath left his body and he died.

His wives and relatives wept bitterly over his needless death. The ancestral spirits in their anger had let him die.

Heroes

Two Boys with Shell Scrapers — Explanation
Told by Sedea and Bauro, March 1967

These two boys always carry shell scrapers, the type still used to pare vegetables if no knife is available. One of the boys is caught by an old cannibal woman and kept as a prisoner in her house. This evil woman also beats the drum, tabu for women.

A talking parrot, rat, and frog assist the boys in vanquishing the old woman. Then a large reward of pigs, porpoise teeth necklaces and other shell valuables is given to the boys.

Typical Baegu ideas found in this tale are the drum tabu, helpful animals, and the emphasis on reward money. Cannibalism is another recurring theme. Once when Sedea was talking about the Baegu war described in the tale *Recent Clan Warfare*, he mentioned that his father had brought back the body of the man killed in battle. They had eaten the body. He described how human flesh was not greasy like that of a pig, but drier. They had also eaten children. "Were they tender?" I asked in a facetious tone. I could hardly believe he was serious. "Yes, they were not tough," he agreed. I stared at him. Startled, I kept staring at him. Suddenly I knew. He was deadly serious. "Sometimes," he continued, "the flesh was cut off the arms and legs while the victim was still alive, and eaten raw. But the ultimate insult was to eat your enemy because you turned him into excrement."

Folktale motifs: Helpful animals
Eating a relative's flesh unwittingly

Two Boys with Shell Scrapers

Two brothers, known by the name Ro Sasata Umari Ki (Two Called Shell Scrapers) because they carried shells of the type used for scrapers wherever they went, picked up their scrapers and went for a hike. Walking along a path, they stopped to scrape the roots of a tree, then noticing it was a fruit tree, an *inikori* tree, they decided to climb it and eat some of the fruit.

After eating the tart green fruit they threw seeds and peelings on the roof of the house below which belonged to Gwaiokibulu, a strange old woman known for her cannibalism. Hearing the noise on her roof, she sent Sisiobulu, her granddaughter, outside to see what was happening. Looking up above the house, Sisiobulu noticed the two boys in the tall fruit tree which her grandmother had forbidden anyone to climb.

Reentering the house, she lied to her grandmother, saying no one was there. Soon the boys threw more fruit skins and seeds on the roof. This time Gwaiokibulu went outside and saw the two boys at the top of the tree. She brought out a large net and placed it around the tree. When the older brother jumped down, she caught him in the net. The younger brother escaped. Gwaiokibulu kept the older boy as a prisoner in her house where she tied him up and told her granddaughter to watch him.

One day as she was leaving the house, she told her granddaughter, "Sisiobulu, if you hear a low pitched drum I have gone to my distant taro garden, but if you hear a high pitched drum I am at my nearby taro garden." Sisiobulu stayed home, heard the low pitched drum, and said, "My grandmother is far away." Suddenly her pet parrot fell toward her crying, "That boy shot me!" The prisoner said, "Let me loose, I shot your parrot." Fearfully, she untied him. Then he asked where the axe was kept that would be used to kill him, and she showed him where it was kept. He ordered her to start building a cooking fire. The younger brother reappeared, and the two of them killed Sisiobulu with the axe. Then they baked her in the fire she had built.

The boys fled into the forest and climbed to the top of a tree named *isimalau*. They made a rope which reached from the top of the tree down to the ground. Then they sharpened sticks and built a fence around the tree trunk before returning to the top of the tree.

Meanwhile Gwaiokibulu, coming back from her taro garden, went into her house and was surprised to find it empty. She opened up the oven, picked up a piece of meat, and began to eat. While eating an arm she suddenly noticed her granddaughter's bracelet. "Those two boys have baked my granddaughter!" she screamed.

Searching for them in the dense forest, she met a frog and asked him if the two boys who had killed her granddaughter had passed his way, but he hadn't seen them. She continued on until she met a huge rat. When she asked him about the two boys, instead of answering her question, he asked, "Are you going to give me a gift?" She promised the rat money, porpoise teeth necklaces, and a pig if he helped her find the boys. The rat replied that since he was a rat, he didn't need or want money. But he gave Gwaiokibulu this advice, " Take eight hairs from your head, put four on one side of your face and four on the other side (like animal whiskers), then walk on the path bordered by cordyline plants where a frog sits in the entrance."

She did as the rat suggested and continued her search. She walked by the tree *isimalau*, looked up, and saw the boys in the treetop. She asked them to throw down a rope because she wanted to climb the tree. They threw down the rope they had made, and she began climbing up. When she had nearly reached the top, they let go of the rope, and Gwaiokibulu fell to the ground. The boys came down and killed the old cannibal woman.

When the boys arrived home, they beat the drum to announce a death. Everyone gathered to find out who had died, and when they heard the evil old Gwaiokibulu had been killed, they brought money, porpoise teeth necklaces, and pigs as rewards to the two boys.

BLACK MAGIC

BLACK MAGIC — EXPLANATION
TOLD BY SEDEA AND BAURO, AUGUST 1967

Wa marries a woman reputed to know black magic. After many years of marriage and the birth of four sons, she finally prays black magic into a portion of his food. He falls under the evil influence of this magic which resides in a snake kept in a hole in the floor of their house. Sympathetic and contiguous magic are used against enemies with the help of this snake.

Women play instrumental roles in the beginning and ending of this tale of black magic. 1. A girl warns against marrying the woman who knows black magic. 2. A women controls the black magic snake. 3. The mother of a victim of the black magic asks for a fighting party to kill the perpetrator of this black magic.

When we first arrived we did not hear about black magic. Later when the subject came up, people claimed to know nothing about it. Then we heard some people had been expelled from our village shortly before our arrival, because they were accused of using black magic. We were there ten months before this story was told.

Once when traveling on a path I dropped a Kleenex and was warned to retrieve it immediately, since it might be picked up and used against me by someone knowing black magic.

People were suspicious and fearful of black magic. The son of the Anglican priest on the coast near us had died about a year earlier. The reason for his death, I was told, was due to black magic, the black magic from the other side of the island where there was plenty of it.

As is frequently found in these tales, money is given to kill an enemy, the usual clan warfare involving blood money. As usual, women are considered to be defiling as seen by the fact that the yam grown by the women's latrine is unfit to be taken to the men's house.

Black lines drawn on each side of Wa's face indicate an altered state when someone is not behaving in the normal way. This idea also appears in *Two Wives* and *Two Boys with Shell Scrapers*.

Wa flouts the custom that bananas and sugarcane are not to be eaten after a death. These foods are not considered to be appropriate when in mourning. Notice in the story *Abunamalao* these foods are given by the spirits.

The area Fau Ro Iu, described earlier, is the location of Wa's unseemly behavior after his relative's death. This captivatingly beautiful place which causes twins seems to be a focus of evil forces.

Folktale motifs: Evil snake
   Magic formulae

BLACK MAGIC

People from five villages asked for forty girls from Robo to meet forty young unmarried men from their villages. This meeting which involved a lot of flirting and looking for marriage partners took place in a beautiful clearing high on Borofunga mountain where red flowering trees were in bloom. While there, one of the girls, Sango Ola, sent this message to Waitao, "Go tell Waitao, son of No, that if he is really a fighting man, he must kill Manoa and take forty pigs in payment." This reward included besides the pigs, shell money, and porpoise teeth, one young girl Kwalumola. Later Sango Ola warned Waitao ,"If you kill Manoa and take the prize money, they will try to marry you to Kwalumola. But do not marry her, because she knows black magic *arua*."

Waitao decided to earn the reward. He visited Manoa in his men's house, and while casually talking to him, suddenly grabbed him by the waist, held him over the fire, and cried to Manoa's brothers, "Eat excrement. This is a murder." Waitao's raiding party, which had accompanied him, heard the dying man's screams and shouted and laughed to drown out the noise. Waitao and his raiding party returned home where the death was announced by drum call. Then he went to Robo to collect the prize. As predicted, after receiving the prize, they led out Kwalumola as a bride, bedecked with ornaments. Waitao having been warned about her, wasn't interested, but his younger cousin Wa said, "If you don't want her, I'll sleep with her." He married her, and over the years she gave birth to four sons.

One day she made a taro and coconut pudding for her four sons. Saving some of it for her husband, she prayed black magic into that portion. Wa ate this pudding and commented that it tasted terrible. That night the black magic spoke to him, "Bring me unripe bananas and a bunch of taro with uncut leaves."

Next morning he told his wife what he had heard in his dream, and she explained that it was black magic from her home. From then on Wa knew the ways of black magic, and his mind began to wander. One day he dug up a yam from the path to the women's latrine and put it in the men's house. It was a defiling object coming from such a place, and if eaten would kill a man. When the men found out where the yam had come from (No's wife had seen him digging it) everyone was furious and accused

Wa of using black magic against them. Wa was angry with No, who had told everyone where his wife had seen Wa digging up the yam. Later when No only gave Wa a tiny piece of the next pig he cooked, Wa was angry again. He sent his sons to get a small piece of something belonging to No. They looked around his house and took half of a betel nut he had momentarily left on the lid of his lime container.

Wa inserted a small sliver of coconut in this betel nut half. Then he went to his bed in back of his house, took off a flat rock covering a hole, and showed the betel nut to his snake which came slithering up from the hole and curled around his left hand. He told the snake to stay away from the betel nut, knowing it would do the opposite. After the snake swallowed the betel nut, by hand Wa forced the betel nut down through the snake's body to its testicles.

While Wa was holding his snake, No was eating more betel nut in his men's house. Suddenly his testicles began to hurt. He cried, "My testicles are almost dead!" He died during the night, and his cousins took his body to the offshore island of Funafou where it was put in the men's house named "One Thousand Men."

Waitao after hearing of his father's death, reclaimed his father's body from the men's house on Funafou and brought it back up the Sasafa River to their home in the hills of Walelangi territory. He buried his father and gave a death feast in his honor. Meanwhile, when Wa heard that No had died, he ground up black rock and with the powder drew black lines on each side of his face. At daybreak with a dancing step he picked up his bow and went out with his sons to a deep, clear pool in the Sasafa, Fau Ro Iu. At night he and his sons put leaves in their hair, danced, and ate foods forbidden after a death, bananas and sugarcane. Waitao could not understand why Wa was rejoicing after No's

Black Magic

death and began to suspect that Wa had used black magic to kill him.

Sometime later, Wa went to a feast and as he watched the dancing, he put a sharp stone at the end of the dance ground. The man leading the dance, Kwataka, stepped on the stone, and the blood from his foot spurted onto a leaf. Wa picked up and kept the leaf. Returning home he noticed Kwaluaru's daughter Latafiala (literally means - sleeps around) working in her garden. Seeing that she left some kindling and a fire stick behind, he cut off a few shreds from both and took them home. He showed these things to his wife, she took the lid off the snake hole and put them inside. The snake ate the leaf, and Kwaitaka, the dancer, died.

Then the snake ate the kindling, and Kwaluaru's daughter died on the same day. Her mother cried bitterly. She suspected Wa since she had seen him secretly watching her daughter working in the garden. She asked her husband, Kwaluaru, to kill Wa since she was sure he had killed their child with his magic.

Kwaluaru offered prize money for the death of Wa. A group of warriors gathered. They sacrificed a pig to insure success of their mission. After they had surrounded Wa's house, Kwaluaru stood by the door and announced, "I have come to take back the souls of No, of Kwataka, and of my daughter, Latafiala, since you killed all three of them with black magic." Then the group of men killed Wa and his wife. Afterward the prize money was collected and distributed to the warriors.

RECENT CLAN WARFARE

A BAEGU WAR — EXPLANATION
TOLD BY BASIA, MARCH 1967

The most modern of these stories, the events described happened during the lives of the grandfathers of the grown men in Ailali village. Basia first told this tale, though it was retold several times and was referred to frequently by many people. It reminded them of their lifestyle before the British pacified the island.

One evening a sample of an all-night singing session *ae ni mae* usually only done during memorial feasts was performed on our verandah. The following story was sung and people became very emotional about it. Tears streamed down some people's faces as they listened intently to the words.

The event described is based on clan warfare. As recorded in other stories, when it was necessary to kill in order to avenge an earlier death of a member of their clan, it was not necessary to kill the murderer, any member of the murderer's clan would do.

In this tale an ambitious mother encourages her son to be a warrior *wane ramo*. Women's status in Malaita is low, but here a mother is exerting pressure on her son behind the scenes.

Magic is called upon to assist the warriors, and to ensure magic will work it continues to be important to be on good terms with ancestral ghosts or spirits.

The ancestral ghost chooses to speak through one of the

warriors. Ancestral ghosts rarely speak, but their all-encompassing presence hovers over many of the characters in these tales. As usual, ancestral ghosts must be attended to and offered pigs at memorial feasts or they will become angry. Note that a feast is properly held at the end of this tale.

Modern elements appear which would not be found in a traditional folktale. The men approach their enemies on a path by the woman's latrine. In more traditional times, no man in his right mind would go near such a path, it would be too defiling. Also rifles as weapons replace the traditional stone axes and spears. Folktale Motif: Magic invisibility

A BAEGU WAR

Kofana and his relatives from Taulangi had killed Maenao, a man from Walelangi (Ailali residents belonged to the Walelangi Clan). When this happened our fathers were not yet grown men. When they were adults their relatives told them about this murder.

Back then Toliala told her son Oofoga, "My child, you should look around in everyone's house in Taulangi while you are free to do so as a child. If when you grow up you are to be a warrior *wane ramo* you must kill a man in Taulangi to avenge the death of your grandfather Maenao. By looking around carefully now, you will know the lay of the land."

After hearing this Oofoga went to the men's house and spoke with his elders, "This is a terrible thing, the death of my grandfather, and my mother says I should seek revenge." After discussing the possibilities for revenge, the elders sent Oofoga and Luiferamo to spy on the village of Taulangi. For three months they spied on this village with the help of special leaves which when sacrificed to certain spirits made them invisible to the people of Taulangi. When they had gathered all the information they wanted, they reported back to their relatives that they thought a fight would end successfully. The elders of Walelangi then decided the battle should begin in seven days. The fighting group of men gathered together and prepared to attack.

In Walelangi when the seventh day arrived, the priest Mautoa brought a sacrificial pig and prayed to the ancestral spirit at Gae saying, "If you are true to me today, you must gather together the men from Taulangi so that they can easily be killed tomorrow." After putting the pig in the fire it bled through the nose, an ominous sign that they would be unsuccessful. However, the noted warrior Luiferamo stood up, stamped his foot, and stated, "Despite this unfavorable sign, I am willing to fight tomorrow."

That evening the entire raiding party gathered to plan the attack. The ancestral ghost from Aenobe spoke through one of the warriors and told him all the men from Taulangi would be sitting in the men's house. Spies were sent to see what was happening in that village, and they saw that all the men were gathered in the men's house as the ancestral ghost had said they would be.

In the middle of the night the warriors surrounded the village of Taulangi. Rakeketo, sitting inside the house spotted one of the spies, and asked if he had come to start a fight. The spy, Maefawai, replied, "This is not a fight. I have come to take back the ghost of my grandfather so his spirit will not disturb the people in your village."

Suddenly a great shout was heard, and the large group of invaders made a surprise attack by rushing up the path by the women's latrine. No one would have expected them by that route since men never walked on a path so defiled. Then Maefawai shot Rakeketo with his rifle. The warriors burned the men's house and killed the occupants, chasing and killing those who tried to escape.

When the victorious warriors arrived home in Walelangi they offered a sacred leaf and a pig to the ancestral ghosts as a thanksgiving for the success of their mission.

THE PIG BEUKWALANGIA

THE PIG BEUKWALANGIA — EXPLANATION
TOLD BY SEDEA AND BAURO, JULY 1967

This tale of a huge pig that travels the length of Malaita mentions many places and characters found in other stories recorded earlier in this book.

Gwaunafilu where this story begins was an important village in Baegu folklore. Kuluabu and Kariomai who were featured in the story *Why Women are Tabu*, and are also in this story, are from Gwaunafilu. *Two Sisters Bulifoia and Fulifoia*, the rebellious daughters, fled from their parents's home in Gwaunafilu. Their mother Taeasi was the sister of Taesalo who was the mother of *Balairi*. It was in Gwaunafilu that Balairi watched the sacred ritual of pig sacrifice. Balairi's sister was Aofunu who in this story also angers the ancestral spirit and causes more problems with pigs. Two men who help chase the pig are the men who discovered taro, Sinakwau and Aokwau. There is an interlocking cast of characters in these folktales and one of the central locations was Gwaunafilu.

This tale of the huge pig begins when Kariomae wants an especially large pig to feed in preparation for the next feast and her husband Kuluabu gives her a pig from the island of Basikana, off the northern coast of Malaita. It grows to be enormous. The name Kariomae gives her huge pig, Beukwalangia, (literally — Swear on Men's House), seems to be asking for trouble.

A young girl, Aufunu, angers the ancestral spirit who then allows this pig, plus others, to escape. But instead of running into the forest as pigs usually do, this one sleeps in a muddy hole by the house where Aufunu sleeps. This is a defiling place for a sacrificial pig to sleep.

Next the pig leads people on a huge chase throughout the length of the island, before it swims to another island, Ulawa, off the southeastern coast of Malaita.

Recurring Baegu themes are the importance of feeding pigs for memorial feasts honoring the ancestors, the defiling presence of women, and the problems that occur when ancestral ghosts are angered.

What is the meaning of this extraordinary pig? He is huge and escapes all who try to capture him. He is polluted from sleeping in a muddy hole next to a woman's house. He comes from as island to the north of Malaita and swims to an island to the southeast of Malaita. He is not a native pig, but passes through the entire island, causing an uproar as he goes.

Translations for the place names where the pig went are given, if known.

Folktale motifs: Supernatural being punishes
breech of tabu
Transformation — pig to rock

THE PIG BEUKWALANGIA

An important man Kuluabu was feeding many pigs in preparation for a feast honoring his ancestors. His wife, Kariamae, wanted him to buy one really large pig to add to the others, so he sent two men to buy a large pig from Tolobasi, who lived on the island of Basikana.

When they returned with the pig, Kuluabu formally presented

The Pig Beukwalangia

it to his wife, handing it to her through the door of her married woman's house. She let the pig run around on the floor of her house and chased after it with a branch of sacred blue cordyline. She named the pig Beukwalangia (literally — Swear on Men's House), and planned for this pig to be the first one of the many to be sacrificed for the feast. She fed the pig well, and he became enormous.

Then a young girl, Aufunu, a relative of Kariamae, picked up the sacred cordyline branch and used it in a cooking fire when she was preparing some taro. This angered the ancestral spirit from Marado who came and spoke to Kuluabu, "Why did this girl use the blue cordyline branch for cooking, this sacred branch over which you intoned my name?" The ancestral ghost continued, "The feast you have been preparing in my honor is not to take place. The pigs will be let loose, other men will eat them. You have not acted correctly toward me. There will be no feast in Gwaunafilu."

So it happened that the pig Alaalaau (Fast Panpipes) and the pig named Fulugagara (Roots Above Ground) escaped into the forest. Next the pig Osikakaro (Without Bamboo Designs) and the pig Gwailabora (Blue Fish) ran away. Then the ancestral spirit let loose the largest pig, Beukwalangia.

This pig instead of running away dug a muddy hole and went to sleep by the wall of the women's house where Aufunu (Unstable Panpipes) and her mother Taeasalo (Sew in the Sky) slept, an improper place for a sacrificial pig to sleep. In the morning Aofunu saw the huge pig and realized it was Beukwalangia. She called out for everyone to help catch this pig and return him to Kuluabu and Kariamae. Many men including Sinakwau and Aokwau (two men who discovered taro) joined the chase.

Soon everyone in Marado was trying to trap this pig. One man crept up and took hold of him, but Beukwalangia shook loose with such force that the group of people around him scattered and fell to the ground. They grabbed the pig again, and he shook them loose a second time. Beukwalangia began leading them on a chase throughout the northern end of Malaita. He went through Luana, then on to Ifumae, then on to Mota, where 50 more people joined the group. They went to Kwakio and Abunarafe (Forbidden Side Road). The chase continued to Akalongora (Snorting Devil) then to Sangisia (Wind Blowing). Next they went to Funugano, then to Asaorana and up the hill to Lakibakwa (Design of Bamboo) then on to Kafoidolo (Eel Water). Next they arrived at Anai, then they followed after the pig to the mouth of the Taeloa River. Picking up more people to join the chase at Suibogi, they continued on to the little Kwara'Ae River. Next they crossed the large Kwara'Ae River. When they arrived at Fauabu (Sacred rock) everyone from Marado gave up and returned home.

Beukwalangia went on alone. He arrived at Anoniu where more people chased him without success. Next he appeared at Regeto, where no one was able to catch him. The pig travelled to Olda, Itialia, and Fauage. He fled on to Faureba (Stone Dance Wand) where more people attempted to capture him. But Beukwalangia ran on to Alasa, then to Maana i Bina (Face of Hornbill) where he slept for two nights.

A strong wind began blowing just before dawn, and Beukwalangia became sick. He jumped into the sea and swam to the beach at Ulawa Island. There he lay down in a sacred place where he died and was changed to a rock.

THE PIG BEUKWALANGIA

Ivens found this large stone sculpture of a pig on the island of Ulawa which was said to have been carved by the Masi (*Melanesians of the Southeast Solomon Islands*, 412.)

BIBLIOGRAPHY

Bauman, Kay, "Shell Ornaments of Malaita," *Art in Small-Scale Societies, Contemporary Readings*, Richard L. Anderson & Karen L. Field, eds, Englewood Cliffs, NJ, Prentice Hall, 1993. Reprinted from *Expedition* 23(2), 1981.

Ivens, Walter G., *Melanesians of the South-East Solomon Islands*, London, Kegan, Paul, French, Trubner, 1927 (reprinted 1972, New York, Benjamin Blom)
Island Builders of the Pacific, London, Seeley, Service 1930.

Keesing, Roger M. *'Elota's Story: The Life and Times of a Solomon Islands Big Man*, St. Lucia U. of Queensland Press, 1978 (reprinted 1983, New York, Holt, Rinehart and Winston) "Ta'a Geni: Women's Perspectives on Kwaio Society," in *Dealing with Inequality*, M. Strathern (ed.) Cambridge, Cambridge U. Press. 1987

Maranda, Elli, "The Myth of Fuusai," in *Folktales Told Around the World*, Richard M. Dorson (ed.) Chicago, University of Chicago Press, 1975,pp. 334-339

Maranda, Pierre, and Elli Köngäs Maranda, "Le Crâne et l'Utérus Deux Théorèms Nord-Malaitans", *Échanges et Communications*, Jean Pouillon et Pierre Maranda (eds.) s'Gravenhague, Netherlands, Mouton 1970, pp.829-61

BIBLIOGRAPHY

Oliver, Douglas L., *A Solomon Island Society*, 1955. Reprinted, Boston, Beacon Press, 1967

Ross, Harold M., *Baegu: Social and Ecological Organization in Malaita, Solomon Islands*, Urbana, University of Illinois Press, 1973

Thompson, Stith, *Motif-Index of Folk-literature*, Bloomington IN, Indiana University Press, Rev. 1989